FOR CHRIS ELIOPOULOS,
MY FRIEND ONCE UPON A TIME,
AND THANKFULLY, WONDERFULLY,
MY FRIEND ONCE MORE.

This is an Arthur A. Levine book

Published by Levine Querido

LQ

LEVINE QUERIDO

www.levinequerido.com • info@levinequerido.com

Levine Querido is distributed by Chronicle Books LLC

Copyright © 2020 by Mike Jung · All rights reserved

Library of Congress Control Number: 2019953557

ISBN: 978-1-64614-011-4

Printed and bound in China.

MIX
Paper from
responsible sources
FSC® C144853

Published October 2020

First Printing

THE **BOYS** IN THE **BACK ROW**

MIKE JUNG

LQ

LEVINE QUERIDO

MONTCLAIR / AMSTERDAM / NEW YORK

 T THE START OF EVERY SCHOOL
year Mom and Dad try to get me all pumped up
by saying things like "it's a whole new year" or
"this is the year when everything changes," which always makes
me think, *uh, no, that was two years ago,* but then sixth grade
came lurching in like a one-legged zombie, and what do you
know, everything actually did change.

Sixth grade would be the year I stopped being "the boy flute
player" and became . . . okay, I didn't stop being the boy flute player
in air quotes, at least inside the band, but I did switch to playing
bass drum for marching band season. Yes, that's me, Matthew
Park, the first boy flute player in the history of Hilltop Summit
K–8 School—not a good thing—and the newest bass drum
player in the Hilltop Summit K–8 School Marching Band. Matt,

to my friends. Friend, I should say, since I only have one for real.

I'd been walking into the band practice room as either "the boy flute player" or "the boy piccolo player" (flute for orchestra, piccolo for marching band) for two years, so it felt very weird to walk into the music wing on the first day of school without an instrument under my arm. It only got weirder to go right past the piccolo players and on to the drum section.

Unlike the piccolo section, the drum section was all guys, which felt a little like entering hostile territory. At least I'd get to sit with my best friend, Eric, though. Wherever he was. Where was he? And why was Sean McKenna looking at me like that? Sean was a snare drummer; why was he playing bass drum? Why was Hector Morales doing that with his hand? Oh right, he had his hand up for a high five.

"Don't leave me hanging," Hector said, grinning so widely that I wouldn't have been surprised if the top half of his head just slid right off the bottom half. I grinned back and smacked his open palm with mine, and looked over the drum line.

"Dude! This is so awesome!" Hector said. "Bass drummers rock!"

"Totally," I said. Well, almost totally. Sean McKenna constantly bragged about his band, his drum kit at home, the concerts his dad took him to, and his girlfriend at another school. Sean did not rock. Hector was okay, though. We liked some of the same movies and stuff, and he didn't talk about himself all the time.

The snare drummers were in the same row at the back of the room as the bass drummers, and were also bunched together like the bass drummers, so it was bass drums, snare drums, and then all the way in the far corner was the tom-tom drummer, Rich Eisen. Rich was a gigantic hulk of an eighth-grader who I actually talked to sometimes, which was a nice change of pace from life with all the other gigantic eighth grade hulks.

Sitting in the middle of the whole drum line, with Rich and the rest of the snare drummers to his right and an empty seat to his left, was Eric Costa, snare drummer, shortest guy in marching band, third-shortest sixth-grade guy at Hilltop Summit K–8 School, and my best friend. Switching from piccolo to bass drum had been his idea, and the whole point of switching was to be in the same section as Eric. That included sitting next to each other on the drum line, but Mr. Radcliffe, history teacher unextraordinaire, made everyone stay late while he finished telling a story about working on an archaeology dig in Copperopolis, wherever that is, so I got to band too late to claim a seat next to Eric. Except it didn't matter, because Eric had saved a seat for me like best friends are supposed to do.

"Thanks for saving me a seat!" I said as I sat down between Eric and Sean, who was staring up at the ceiling. Sean tilted his head a little, gave me kind of a nod as if I was thanking him, then turned his eyes back to the ceiling. "Mr. Radcliffe was . . . you know, being himself."

"No worries," Eric said as he put an arm across my shoulders and pretended to punch me in the arm. He nodded toward Sean and Hector. "I had to tell these slackers to move over, but they know who's boss."

Sean snorted. "Yeah, right."

"Dude, you're boss, but you're not *the* boss," Hector said cheerfully.

"You're the only person I know who uses 'boss' like that," Eric said.

"That's because I'm boss too," Hector said. I jumped when he reached over Sean's hunched shoulders and tapped *my* shoulder, right next to Eric's hand.

"Bass drummer selfie!" Hector said, holding a phone up at arm's length and leaning into Sean. He grinned at Eric. "Not you, bro, sorry!"

Eric laughed and lifted his arm up and away from me.

"Dude, get *off* me," Sean said, jostling Hector with an elbow. He didn't lean out of the way of the picture, though.

"What, no selfie stick?" I said as I smiled, Sean held up a hand with his index finger and pinkie pointing up, and Hector took the pic.

"I wish."

"I'm just kidding."

"I'm not!"

I turned back to Eric.

"Dude," he said. "This is the best."

"It's better than the best!"

"Well, no. Nothing's better than the best—that's why they call it 'the best.'"

"What about 'the bestest'?"

Eric did a super-exaggerated, obviously fake eye roll, and I laughed, just because it was the first day of school and being in the drum section with Eric was already the best. Or the bestest.

The door to the music office opened, and the band director, Mr. Drabek, strolled through it with his conducting baton in hand.

"Hello, musicians!" Mr. Drabek said as everyone but me was still secretly looking at their phones. You can't secretly look at a phone you don't have. "Get ready to make some noise!"

There were a few cheers—real cheers, not sarcastic ones. Band geeks tend to like that rah-rah, hooray-for-us stuff. Drabek nodded.

"Listen up! Horns and bass drums have a lot of new players, so we have a lot of work ahead of us, but before we get started, I have some big news."

Big news on the very first day of school? INTERESTING. Everyone instantly shut up.

Mr. Drabek clasped his hands behind his back, grinned, and rocked back on his heels, clearly having fun by dragging things out.

"SO WHAT IS IT?" Hector said, drawing a bunch of laughs.

"Oh sorry, I was just enjoying the quiet," Mr. Drabek said cheerfully. "I'm not so used to that. The big news is that in the fall I sent in an application for a certain music festival that takes place in May, and to make a long story short, we're going to perform in the World of Amazement Spring Festival for the first time!"

The room erupted in cheers.

"We're going to World of Amazement? Like, on a field trip?" Hector yelled.

"Yes, we are, and hey, no yelling," Mr. Drabek said.

World of Amazement was the best amusement park in the state—the biggest roller coaster, the best video games, the most swimming pools, and the coolest gift shops. It was huge, practically a small city of its own, and every year it did a super-fancy spring music festival with tons of decorations, gigantic light displays, and performances by choirs, dance troupes, cheerleaders, and all kinds of bands from all kinds of schools. Everyone started babbling about whatever time it was they'd gone there (Mom and Dad took Eric and me in fifth grade; it was so awesome) or about how their families were totally planning on going but now they didn't have to.

"Okay, settle down, settle down," Mr. Drabek said, waving his hands over his head. "This will affect our schedule for the whole year, because the festival's in May, and we definitely want to be at our best when we get there. So, we're going to have our normal fall marching band season, then have a shortened spring orchestra season so we can get some extra marching rehearsal in before traveling."

There was an "aww" or two, and a few scattered boos, but

most people were obviously fine with that. I mean, seriously, World of Amazement! I'd skip *all* of spring orchestra for that, and I really like orchestra.

"It's really exciting and it's going to be a lot of fun, but it's also going to be a lot of work, because we can't wait until the spring to lay our foundation—we need to start doing that now. We're going to rehearse like we've never rehearsed before. Buckle up!"

I held out a hand, palm up, and Eric smacked it with his hand, palm down. The Blue Beetle emergency signal ring on his finger caught the light, and Sean turned his head and looked at it for a second.

I picked up my mallets, craned my neck over my drum to look at Mr. Drabek, and had a super-fast moment of panic. What the heck was I doing? I was a woodwind player, not a drummer! I got it under control pretty fast, though. I knew how to play real music, with pitch and dynamics and everything; the bass drum didn't even need to be tuned. Piece of cake, right?

I **ALSO DIDN'T KNOW HOW TO PLAY FLUTE**
or piccolo at first, of course, but I got pretty good at both.
Playing them was Dad's idea. When he said, "You should
start playing a musical instrument—what do you think about
the flute?" during the summer before fourth grade, I said, "Okay,
sure," not knowing anything about band, band instruments,
who played which band instruments, and the dangers of picking
the wrong instrument—I only knew Dad used to play the flute
too. He still had his old flute stuffed into a closet. Why not be
like Dad and be a flute player? What's the worst that could
happen?

I had no idea, and it's not like Dad would have said anything
about playing a "girl's instrument" unless he'd had a brain trans-
plant. I still remembered the summer after second grade (before

we moved) when we were at the beach with our cousins. Uncle David said I should stop playing with my cousin Rebecca's beach toys because "boys don't play with pink toys," and Dad kind of got into it with him. Dad called Uncle David a knuckle-dragger, and Uncle David called Dad a girlyman. It might have been funny if it hadn't been for the super-intense way they stared at each other, even though they both pretended to be joking.

Uncle David hasn't visited us in a while.

Mom also didn't believe in "boy instruments" or "girl instruments," whether I was the only boy flute and piccolo player in school or not. Every single bully at school disagreed with them, though, and they didn't tell Mom and Dad about it. They told me, sometimes with their big smelly mouths, and sometimes with their big smelly fists. At least my tolerance for pain has gone up, haha.

I liked the flute, though, even with all the extra harassment it got me. I liked its silvery look, and the cushiony sound the pads made when I pressed the keys down. I liked the extra raised part on the mouthpiece that your lip rested on, and the one key that needed to be played with your thumb. I liked the piccolo too—it was small enough to easily carry around with one hand, and the whole instrument case fit into my backpack with room to spare.

I also liked playing the same instrument Dad had played. We didn't really have anything else like that.

I took the flute to school on the first day of fourth grade at Hilltop Summit K–8 School, ready to join the orchestra at Mom's suggestion. My flute wasn't super fancy or anything, but it was brand-new, and I'd polished it until it practically glowed in the dark. I walked into the band room, looked for the flute section, and found myself sitting in the middle of a giant mob of girls. I was the only boy in the whole section. Some kids actually took pictures of me with their phones.

The music room was kind of like a theater—the floor had three different tiers, highest in the back (where all the storage closets were) and lowest in the front (where the whiteboard and the biggest empty space was). The flute section (and during marching band season, the piccolo section) was right in the front. Some of the flute players looked at me like I'd just stepped out of a flying saucer, but they also seemed friendly, and a bunch of them smiled or made little waving motions with one hand.

There were at least a dozen flute players, and that was only the fourth- and fifth-grade band! How many flute players were there in sixth, seventh, and eighth grades? A thousand? Two thousand?

"Uh . . . hi," I said.

"Hi!" a girl I was standing next to said. She was older than me, probably in fifth grade, and was one of a handful of Asian kids in the room. "Are you new?"

"Yeah," I said. "I'm Matt."

"Skye Oh," she said, sticking out her hand. Very businesslike. We shook.

"So, wow, you play the flute!" Skye said.

"Well, I'm just starting," I said. "Why do you say 'wow'?"

"We've never had a boy who plays flute before."

Hmm. That was new information.

"How long is never?"

"Well, my sister's in sixth grade—she's over there in the saxophone section—and my brother—over there in the clarinet section—is in fifth grade. I've seen all their performances, and the flute section has always been all girls. That's so cool that you play anyway!"

"Thanks, I guess." I rubbed the back of my head and looked around the room. The flute section wasn't just all girls, it was almost all white girls. There were a few nonwhite faces scattered throughout the rest of the room—Skye, her sister, an Asian boy who looked like Skye and was the only oboe player in the room, and a brown kid in the drum section—but mostly the band was super, super white. The whole school was like that, so at least the band was being consistent.

Gah. Sometimes I wonder if I'd be happier without my parents always pointing out stuff like that, because I can't not see it any-more. I guess it's better to know, but that doesn't make it happier to know.

"You should sit down," Skye said, tilting her head behind me. I turned to see a door with a glass window in it, and "MUSIC OFFICE" in green letters on the glass. A teacher with a mus-tache and a green sweater appeared in the window and opened the door. I scanned for an empty seat with the other flute players, but there weren't any, which was funny since in any other class-room the empty seats would ALL be in the front. I panicked a little and bolted for the back of the room, ending up in a seat next to a short white kid who was silently drumming a pair of sticks against his leg. He smiled at me and pointed at my chest with one drumstick.

"I like your shirt," he said.

I looked down at my chest, which was covered by an illustra-tion of Beethoven Yoo, Bella Underwood, Petra and Hex Ursu (they're twins), and Kofi Bedichek, aka the Rocket Cats. A lot of people make fun of my Rocket Cats shirt, not knowing how awesome and superheroic the Cats really are, so it was cool to get some positive attention for it.

"Thanks," I said. "Do you—"

"Good morning, musicians!" Mr. Drabek said, standing in the front of the room. "Get ready to make some noise!"

"—read comics?" I said, switching into a whisper and turning to face Mr. Drabek.

"Not really," the drummer kid whispered back, sitting up really straight and putting a very I'm-paying-attention expression on his face.

"Okay, let's get reorganized—flutes here, clarinets here," Drabek said, pointing first at the place where most of the flute players already were, then at the area next to them. "Saxophones there, horns there, percussion in the back . . ."

"You play flute, huh?" Drummer Kid said.

"Yeah. I guess I'll be playing piccolo in marching band."

"Cool."

"I didn't know the flute section would be all girls . . ."

Drummer Kid shrugged.

"So what?"

I smiled. *Yeah, so what?*

"I like most of the flute players," he said. "The trumpet section, on the other hand . . . You know what, you should probably go find a seat."

"Yeah, I guess. Hey, I'm Matt."

Drummer Kid stuck out his hand. "I'm Eric."

"Dude, only girls play the flute!" the kid on the other side of Eric said. He still had his phone in his hand, and he took a picture of my shirt and grinned to himself as he stuck the phone into the pocket of his jeans.

"Does everyone in this school have their own phone?" I said, pressing my hand down on my pocket with no phone in it.

"Shut up, Sean," Eric said, making a shooing motion over his shoulder.

"There's no way you'd ever catch me playing a girl's instrument," Sean said. He twirled a drumstick in his fingers, rock star style, but then dropped it with a clatter.

"Hey, do you want to read some comic books?" I said to Eric, deciding to ignore Sean.

"Yeah, sounds like fun."

"Cool."

"Comic books are okay," Sean said to the back of my head. "If you're into that kind of thing."

"Find a seat, everyone, let's go," Mr. Drabek said. I hustled down to the front of the room to take my place with the girls and their girl instruments.

I was definitely having doubts about my choice of instrument, but Skye turned out to be awesome—she was good at giving advice in a way that didn't make you feel stupid—and after the first practice I realized I was already one of the better players in the section. It helped that we were playing reeeeeeeally basic stuff, but still, I knew right away that I wasn't totally horrible at the music thing. Plus I might have already made two friends, Eric and Skye. A person can dream, anyway.

My first-ever band practice went by at warp speed, and when it was over everyone packed up and headed for the band room exit in a noisy stampede. The door to the rest of the music wing was along one side of the risers where the band sits, kind of like the hallway leading into an upstairs movie theater. Our cubbies were there too, and a super-tight traffic jam formed as everyone tried to get their stuff out of their cubby at the same time. In the crush of band geeks I got pushed shoulder to shoulder with Eric, who grinned and rolled his eyes.

"Welcome to the cattle pen," he said.

"Is it like we're being led to slaughter?"

"Feels like that, doesn't it?"

"Is this normal?" I said. I could actually feel people squished up against my chest, back, both shoulders, and both arms.

"I'd say no, but I'd be lying."

"Hey, are you a girl?" an older kid said, sticking his face right between Eric's head and my head. I got a blast of his warm, horrible breath right in the face, and I jerked my head sideways and almost knocked my skull against the shoulder of a tall girl who I later found out was named Janet Fritz. Janet's really tall.

That was my introduction to Kenny Delacroix. It was like crossing a bridge and finding out there was a mean, trumpet-playing troll with a terrible sense of humor living under it.

"I said, are you a girl? Or are you just gay?"

"Oh shut up, Ken," Eric said. "You're such an idiot."

"If you're asking for a kiss, the answer's no," I said, surprising myself. Eric grinned at me over his shoulder, and there was a burst of laughter from the band geek pileup around me. Kenny's super-hairy eyebrows went up in surprise.

"Show him who's boss, Kenny," Sean said from behind me.

"No means no, Kenny!" a girl's voice said from somewhere else in the human pileup—I wasn't sure, but I think it might have been Skye's sister—but Kenny ignored it and leaned in even closer to me. We were practically cheek to cheek.

"Oh, you're dead, Wang," he said.

"My last name's Park."

"Your name's Wang, Wang." Kenny poked me in the back with a finger, hard, on each "Wang."

"Racist much?" Eric said to the back of Kenny's head. "And what does that even mean?"

"I'm not talking to you, midget, I'm talking to the Chink."

"I'm not Chinese," I said.

"You're whatever I say you are, Wang!"

"You're an idiot," Eric said, waving Kenny away like a fly.

A gap opened in the layer of people in front of me, and I turned sideways and slithered through it, away from Kenny and his disturbing finger. Lucky for me the only thing in my cubby was my backpack. I pulled it out, escaped into the hallway where the mob scene was a little more spread out, and booked it down the hallway, feeling bummed out and angry.

"Don't worry about it," someone said. I looked up to see Sean walking next to me.

"Don't worry about what?" I said, confused because I hadn't done anything to Sean.

"About what Kenny said—he's just being fur

"He was being *what*?" I stopped and turned my w.

look at Sean, who surprised the crap out of me by stickı.

hand straight at me. I grabbed it mostly to keep it from poking

me in the chest.

"I'm Sean, by the way. Sean McKenna."

He squeezed my hand once, hard, then dropped it.

"Is that Kenny person a friend of yours?" I said. "Because he's

pretty racist."

"Yeah, we're buds, and nah, he's not a racist," Sean said, wav-

ing off what I'd said like it was nothing, even though it was defi-

nitely *not* nothing. "See you later."

Sean McKenna, having weirdly introduced himself with both

of his names, strolled away.

"Hey, Matt!"

I looked over my shoulder and saw Eric hurrying toward

me with his backpack on and a pair of drumsticks in his

hands.

"I see you've met Tweedledum *and* Tweedledee," Eric said.

"What a couple of jerks," I said as we headed out of the music

wing. "Does Kenny know this is the twenty-first century?"

"I'm sure he doesn't care," Eric said.

"Well, if he was trying to ruin my first time at band practice, it worked."

"He's good at ruining stuff."

"And what's with that Sean kid?" I asked. "He was all, 'Kenny's not a racist' and 'I'm Sean McKenna,' like I'd know who he is."

"Sean's super annoying," Eric said. "He's not as bad as Kenny, though. So, hey, were you serious about the comic book thing?"

It was my turn to grin, although I secretly felt worried, like, what if this kid finds out I'm actually a giant dork? It was a legit worry, even if it wasn't a new worry.

"Totally!" I said. "Can you come over to my house after school today?"

"Yeah, let's go!"

So, after school we headed off to Chez Park, dork strong, united by harassment, already in the process of becoming best friends. In the end, fourth grade turned out to be pretty good, because how many times a year do you meet your best friend in the whole world?

O YEAH, THAT WAS FOURTH GRADE.
Two years later Kenny was still terrorizing anyone
who he thought was gay, weaker than him, smarter
than him, smart at all, or different from him in any visible way,
and Sean was still walking the line between being truly evil and
being just annoying.

Telling Mom and Dad about the competition would be
easy—if there was music, art, theater, or writing involved, they
were automatically on board. I totally expected them to say yes.
A half hour after Eric went home we had dinner, where Mom
and Dad did their usual comedy routine about weird food.

"Hey, did you finish off the quinoa?" Dad said.

"Yup," Mom said.

"Honey, you know I'm not eating grains," Dad said. "Come on."

"What's that have to do with it?"

"Quinoa's a seed. I'm not cutting down on seeds."

"I see you're not cutting down on mansplaining either."

"Yes, sorry, mansplaining's even unhealthier than eating carbs," Dad chuckled in his gee-whiz-I'm-funny way.

Yes, this is the kind of stuff my parents talk about. Quinoa. Kale. How to ruin perfectly good muffins by making them with almond flour and coconut oil. MUFFINS SHOULD BE MADE WITH REGULAR FLOUR. It was amazing how many websites and blogs Mom and Dad could find with instructions for ruining perfectly good food by making it all "paleo." Lucky for me, Dad is actually willing to cook stuff I like, so if there was going to be any trouble during dinner, it wouldn't be because I hated the food. If there was going to be trouble, it'd be because I said how relieved I was to not hear jokes all day about playing a girl's instrument.

At least I'm not mansplaining, I thought. Mansplaining's when a man (like Dad) tries to explain something to a woman (like Mom) who already knows about the thing. They talk about stuff like that too. Mom and Dad have really confusing conversations.

"So Mom, Dad—"

"Uh-oh," Dad said. "'So,' huh?"

"Right, nothing good ever starts with 'so,'" Mom said with a grin.

"You guys are so funny," I said. "Or at least you think you are."

"Come on, Matt, spit it out." Dad handed me the bowl of Parmesan before I asked, and I shook a bunch of it onto my bowl of farfalle.

"The marching band's entered in a competition at World of Amazement," I said.

"Really!" Dad said. "That sounds great!"

"Wonderful, we're in," Mom said. "How much do you need?"

See? Mom and Dad are awesome, despite their terrible sense of humor.

"I don't know yet. They're gonna hand out the forms and stuff later in the month," I said. "So it's okay if I go?"

"A marching band competition at World of Amazement? Are you kidding?" Dad said with a laugh. "Of course it's okay!"

"Are you sure?"

"Geez, Matt, do you want to go?" Dad said.

"Are you asking us, or are we asking you?" Mom said.

"I'm asking."

"YES," Mom and Dad said in unison. I don't know how they do that, but it's kind of impressive. Also kind of creepy.

"Okay. Thanks."

"I just wish . . ." Dad said.

"No you don't," Mom said.

"I haven't said anything yet," Dad said, raising his arms in protest.

"No, but starting with 'I just wish' never ends well."

". . . Sometimes it does," Dad said.

"Nope." Mom shook her head.

Mom and Dad had this argument all the time, so it didn't distract me from feeling like I knew what Dad was "just wishing."

"I was just going to say it would be meaningful if you'd play piccolo at the competition—"

Knew it.

"—but I still support you in playing the instrument you want to play."

Mom, who'd been sitting with arms crossed and a twisty-mouth, wiggly-eyebrow kind of look on her face, smiled and patted him on the arm.

"Nicely done, honey."

"DON'T PATRONIZE ME, WOMAN," Dad said in a super-deep voice. "I AM A MAN!" He stuck out his chest so far it looked like an alien was about to burst out of it.

Mom and I took our time snorting, hooting, and saying things like "What??" and "Yeah, *right*," while Dad laughed with us. Mom stuck her tongue out at Dad, but she also put a hand on his arm. He grabbed her hand, brought it to his lips, and kissed it. They're so gross sometimes.

"I know, Dad," I said. "I'm sorry, I just—"

"No no no no no," Dad said, waving the hand that Mom wasn't still holding. "*I'm* sorry, this is my issue, not yours."

"I'm glad Eric and I will be in the same section for this," I said. "It'll be, like, you know, the biggest marching band adventure we'll have together."

"Aw, you guys are adorable!" Mom said. I guess it was too adorable for her to keep sitting down, because she actually stood up and hugged me around the neck, even though she was in the process of eating a piece of kale.

"Kale, Mom. Kale in my hair."

"Oh sorry!" Mom looked at the half piece of kale she'd just mashed against the side of my head and brushed the crumbled bits off into her hand.

"That is so sweet, Matt," Dad said with a smile. "Of course you'd want to do that. Especially now that you're in the same section!"

Even though I'm not playing the flute like you want me to! And I feel terrible about it! A little bit angry too! Also I feel incredibly wrong for feeling terrible and angry about it! I'm the biggest dork on the planet—no wonder Eric's my only friend!

"It sounds perfect," Dad said. "Will there be a day to get out and have some fun while you're there? Maybe get to know some of the kids from the other marching bands?"

"Yeah," I said. "The last day we get to go on the rides and stuff."

"It's a done deal, honey, don't you worry about it," Mom said. "How was your first day playing bass drum?"

"It was fun," I said, pangs of guilt still going through me. "Bass drum's kind of easy, actually."

"You're probably banging out quarter notes most of the time," Dad said, pretending to hit a drum with alternating swings of his fists.

"Kind of," I said. "It's fun, but it's really different from piccolo."

"Well, it'll give you a good head start on playing drums in orchestra," Dad said. His voice was so ridiculously cheerful that he sounded like an anime character, and Mom caught his eye and smiled. I know she thinks I don't notice that kind of stuff, like I'm always looking out the window or something.

"Hopefully," I said. "I'll still need to practice, though."

"I'm not so sure about having a drum kit in here," Dad said with a smile.

"Me neither," Mom said.

"I mean at school."

"Ah, okay," Dad said.

"Remember that time we went to the Pop Culture Museum and I played the drums in their sound lab?" Mom said. "I was pretty good."

Dad and I nodded in agreement. Mom had rhythm.

"The thought of both of you practicing doesn't make me think a drum kit in here will be, you know, quieter," Dad said.

"Me neither, I'm just thinking out loud," Mom said. "Matt, I love that you had the self-confidence to be the only boy in a section full of girls, whether you decide to go back to it or not . . ."

Mom ruffled my hair. Self-confidence? What did that have to do with anything? "Lack of advance warning" was more like it. And was she really rubbing my hair with a hand that had hummus on it? Yes, she was.

"Mom. You need to use a napkin."

"Oops, sorry, honey. I'm just saying, if you want to keep playing drums, we can probably figure something out." She looked at Dad. "What do you think, honey?"

"Thanks for asking, honey!" Dad said, sounding only a little bit sarcastic. "I'm still not sure, but they do have those electronic drum kits where the sound all comes through headphones."

"Mom. Dad. I don't even know what I'd play in orchestra yet. Calm down."

They both laughed.

"Sorry, sorry," Mom said.

"Too much pressure, I know," Dad said. He got up, walked around the table, and gave me a kiss on the top of the head.

"A little bit," I said, but I let him kiss my head anyway.

"We're thrilled about the competition, it sounds wonderful," Mom said.

"Awesome. Hey, since I'll be spending a whole weekend in another city, can I get a phone?"

"NO," Mom and Dad said together.

Rats.

I T WAS WEIRD TO THINK ABOUT PRAC-
ticing for an event that was months and months away,
and at first I was pretty nervous about playing a new
instrument at World of Amazement because I'd never played in
front of such a gigantic audience before. Mr. D didn't actually
talk about WoA that much, though, and as the first weeks of
school went by I got sucked into the process of adjusting to my
new gig.

In some ways, playing the bass drum was super easy com-
pared to playing the piccolo. There aren't any notes, you don't
have to worry about staying in tune, and most of the time you're
just banging on the drum one beat at a time. In other ways, it
was harder—the drums are bigger and heavier, and I actually did
get a little bored by banging out quarter notes.

On the plus side, when a song got all fortissimo it was fun to hammer on the drums really hard. Also, the view from the drum section was way better than from the piccolo section. The piccolos are at the front of the band room, so we—I mean they—have to turn around to see anything interesting that's happening, but the drums are at the back of the room. Each of the band room's three levels was as high as one step on a staircase, with the highest tier at the back, which meant we could see everything going on in the room without having to hear it first, then turn around and look.

From up there it was obvious that a bunch of kids were really good at secretly checking their phones, the clarinet section was rowdier than I thought it was, and most of the girls and at least one of the boys in the band spent a lot of time staring dreamily at Summer Oh's brother Graysin as he adjusted the mouthpiece on his clarinet. He *is* really good-looking, to be fair. Then I looked over at the trumpet section and realized *two* boys were staring at Graysin. One was the newest trumpet player, and the other was . . . Kenny?

Kenny hadn't even taken his trumpet out of its case yet—it was in his lap, with his giant troll hands resting on top of it, and he was definitely staring at Graysin. His face looked weird—sad, maybe—then he caught my eye, and for a second he almost looked scared. Then he made a terrifying "I'm going to kill you" face, and I quickly looked away.

Bass drum was easy enough to play that by October I was already getting a handle on the other bass drummers. Hector was definitely not great—he missed a lot of notes, and he spent a lot of time staring at the music with a frown—but the real problem turned out to be Sean. He was terrible! He always talked about his drum kit at home and the band he was in, and he'd played snare the year before, but he couldn't stay on the beat to save his life. Unlike Hector, however, he didn't just drop out—he played really loudly, which made it super hard on those of us who were actually playing the songs right. At one point he looked over at me and shook his head, a clear "dude, that was wrong" message, even though he'd messed it up and I'd gotten it right!

"Okay, gang, that's it," Mr. Drabek said at the end of class. "New horns and bass drummers, you're doing solid work, but there's definitely a lot of tightening up to do—"

"Totally," Sean said in a firm, loud voice. Grrr.

"—before the Spring Festival, but overall, that's a good start. Thanksgiving parade's in six weeks, and starting next time we'll rehearse outside until the holiday break, so start dressing warmly. Go home!"

He did a big waving motion with his baton, and the room was suddenly all scraping chairs, rustling papers, and snapping latches as everyone hurried to put their stuff away. I manhandled my drum back into its spot in the closet, getting there before both Hector and Sean. Sean looked like he was going to say something to me, but as he opened his mouth I turned sideways, my back facing him and my front facing Hector, and slithered between them.

"Dude, that rocked!" Hector said as he lowered his bass drum to the floor in front of him.

"It did!" I paused and leaned back to accept his high five. "See you tomorrow."

"Definitely."

"This is awesome!" Eric said when I was done running the bass drum gauntlet.

"Totally," I said, meaning the "we're in the same section" part and the "World of Amazement" part, not the "Sean is really bad at drums" part. "You want to draw after school today?"

"Yup." Eric grinned. "So, your house?"

"Sure. How come we never go to your house anymore?"

"All the comics are at your house."

"What are you talking about? You have comics, you have a whole collection."

"Yeah, but you had a head start. There are MORE comics at your house."

"Huh. Good point. Okay, my house, then."

"Cool. I gotta grab some stuff out of my locker—"

"Me too."

"Dude." Eric grinned. "This is gonna be awesome."

"Totally," I said. "Best field trip ever."

I, DAD," I SHOUTED AS ERIC AND I came in through the front door and dropped our backpacks on the floor.

"Hey, buddy," Dad said, walking out of the kitchen with his laptop balanced in one hand as Eric and I kicked off our shoes. He gave me a one-armed sideways hug and a kiss on the side of the head, and I leaned into him for a couple of seconds.

"Hi, Mr. Park," Eric said as he pushed his shoes around with one foot. Dad lifted his non-laptop arm off my shoulder and over my head, then squeezed Eric's shoulder.

"What do you gentlemen have planned today?" Dad said.

"Homework," I said. Dad snorted in his usual "I'm not a fan of homework" way as he pushed around a messy pile of envelopes on the entryway table. Seriously, Dad *hates* homework—he even writes blog posts about it.

"There's a book by an author named Greg Pincus you guys should read. It's called *The Homework Strike*—"

"Read it," Eric and I said at the same time. All three of us cracked up.

"Ah, here it is." Dad fished an envelope out of the pile and waved it at us. "My new ACLU membership card, boys. Important stuff."

"Awesome," Eric said, giving me a squirmy-eyebrow, "what does that mean" look. I mouthed "tell you later" back at him as Dad tucked the envelope into his shirt pocket.

"Dad, are you fighting with people on the internet again?"

"Yes," Dad said, tucking the envelope into his armpit and poking at his laptop's touch pad. "You guys shouldn't do it, though. You don't, right?"

"Nope," Eric said, lying like an expert.

"Well . . . ," I said, which got me a look from Dad. "Oh, COME ON, Dad, look who's talking!"

"Yes, yes, you're right," Dad said as all three of us headed for the kitchen. "I understand things get pretty heated on the Sandpiper Network."

"You know about the Sandpiper Network?" Eric said.

"I do."

Whatever the word is for feeling totally proud of your dad and totally embarrassed by him at the same time is the word for how I felt right then. At least it was Eric—with anyone else it would have been 100 percent humiliation.

"We have stuff to do, Dad," I said, grabbing Eric's elbow and pulling him toward the basement door, which was next to the side door of the house.

"Sadly, I do too," Dad said. "I got some macaroons, if you guys are interested. In the fridge."

"Not coconut," I said, letting Eric head downstairs first.

"Yes, coconut."

"Er, no thanks," I said as I closed the door behind me and hustled down the staircase. I heard Dad say "your loss" as I got to the bottom.

Living in the basement of my mom and dad's house means living with a giant pole in the middle of the room, super-cold temperatures in winter, and tons of static electricity from the thousand-year-old carpet. Also, the laundry room was down there, so Mom made a lot of trips up and down the stairs to do laundry and yell at me for not helping more with laundry. But it was my bedroom, all mine, so I wasn't complaining. Much.

Eric and I were way into this comic book artist named Jonah Burns—he drew Rocket Cats, League of Infamy, The Flammables, and a bunch of other stuff—but our favorite comic book character of his was Sandpiper. She didn't have any superpowers, but she was smarter and a better fighter than anyone else, and Burns drew the best fight scenes. I was always impressed by the way he drew Sandpiper's feet, especially when she was kicking someone in the jaw. *Sandpiper* was also the comic book I gave Eric to read the first time he came over to my house, back in fourth grade.

There's a mini-size door leading into a space under the stairs, which contains the greatest treasure in the Park household: my comic book collection. In fourth grade I only had about two hundred total issues, but by sixth grade it was over six hundred, mostly because everyone knew comic books were the only present I ever wanted. I had the entire twelve-issue run of *Miss Missile*; the first issue of *Captain Stupendous*, before they changed the color of his cape from black to yellow (a birthday present from Uncle Doug); and every issue of *Infinite Comics Team-Up*, including the one with Velocity Girl and Sonic Boom.

We sat down in front of my desk, which was actually just a big folding table covered with piles of my stuff, and stared at the screen of my laptop as I hit the enter key and woke it up from sleep mode.

"So I feel kind of weird about getting on the Sandpiper Network after your dad talked about it," Eric said. "Like he might actually be there, pretending to be a fan."

"Uh, yeah, that is *super* paranoid," I said as I logged in.

"About your dad, maybe, but remember that guy who pretended to be a teenage girl?"

"So are you gonna delete your account?"

Eric snorted. "No!" He held up his phone, showing me the login screen for the SN app.

"Me neither."

Sandpiper Network was just one of the chat rooms hosted by Vertex, which used to be "Vertex Comics" until their first superhero movie came out and earned fifty quadrillion dollars and it became just plain "Vertex," which I guess makes sense since they're also a movie studio and toy seller and all that other stuff. There's actually a lot of other stuff besides the chat rooms—the fan fiction site is huge, and the Vertex Compendium has enough information about all the Vertex superheroes to make your head explode—but Sandpiper Network's where to go to seriously talk with other serious fans. The thing that's hard about SN is how many people use it—when it's quiet, there might only be five or six people there. When it's busy, there might be as many as twenty people there, which makes it kind of hard to follow the conversation.

I logged in and discovered it was a very, very, very busy day.

FelineAvenger has entered the chat. themightymightyEric, Pooper-man, pollywantablaster, invulneraBill, makimochi, iamthedissident, and 174 others are already here.

A HUNDRED AND SEVENTY-FOUR? What??

"Whoa," Eric said. "Are you seeing this?"

"Yeah."

"I can't keep up!"

The chat was scrolling by so fast that we couldn't even say anything at first—we just read as fast as we could.

POLLYWANTABLASTER: so awesome

INVULNERABILL: is it an omnibus?

POOPERMAN: it's an iconic edition

VIGILANTEINUNDERPANTIES: whats an iconic edition

FASTBALLSPECIAL: like an awesome omnibus

VINCENTWU: its a new thing

IAMTHEDISSIDENT: what's defendercon

INVULNERABILL: a con

ZOMBIESQUIRREL: why is it Sandpiper, i hate her

POLLYWANTABLASTER: Sandpiper's the best

ZOMBIESQUIRREL: shes the worst

POLLYWANTABLASTER: you're the worst

IAMTHEDISSIDENT: haha, you should call yourself notfun-nyabill

MAKIMOCHI: it's a small conference

CANDYCANECHRISSY: omg its so expensive

INVULNERABILL: no its not

FASTBALLSPECIAL: why are u so mean bill

MAKIMOCHI: that's how much cons cost

INVULNERABILL: why are you so annoying

CANDYCANECHRISSY: i mean the iconic Sandpiper

ZOMBIESQUIRREL: girl superheroes are a waste of time

POLLYWANTABLASTER: you're a waste of time

POOPERMAN: hey the cons right next to world of amaze-ment

ZOMBIESQUIRREL: so you hate all boys it figures

POLLYWANTABLASTER: no, just you

FelineAvenger: wait what??

FASTBALLSPECIAL: polly hates zombiesquirrel

THEMIGHTYMIGHTYEric: he means world of amazement

ZOMBIESQUIRREL: shut up slowballspecial

FASTBALLSPECIAL: what an amazing burn #irony

POLLYWANTABLASTER: defendercon's at the Soerio Center,
   it's really close to WoA

IAMTHEDISSIDENT: where are the mods when you need em

FelineAvenger: but what's happening at defendercon?

POLLYWANTABLASTER: the Sandpiper Iconic Edition launch
   with Jonah Burns

THEMIGHTYMIGHTYEric: he'll be there?

POLLYWANTABLASTER: yup

INVULNERABILL: duh, it's a signing

FASTBALLSPECIAL: youre such a jerk, vulneraball

FelineAvenger: WHEN is it?

MAKIMOCHI: end of May

POLLYWANTABLASTER: may 25

Eric and I looked up from our screens and stared at each other in real space.

"Dude," Eric said. "*May 25.* Is that—"

I was already pawing through the papers on my desk like a wild animal.

"I think it is, I think—" I pulled a paper from the stack and held it up. "Here!"

My copy of the World of Amazement flyer was a little crumpled, but it was still easy to see the giant header at the top that said "World of Amazement Spring Festival" and the dates right underneath it:

May 23–25.

"Holy crap," I said. "That's . . ."

"Yeah," Eric said. "The same time as our field trip."

ONAH BURNS!" I SLAMMED THE SHEET of paper back down on my desk and almost fell out of my chair. "In the same city AND at the same time as our field trip! What are the odds??"

"Well, you know," Eric said. "Super, super low. But not impossible."

"Obviously, since it's actually happening!"

"The timing couldn't be worse." Eric was sliding lower and lower in his chair. Gloom was practically oozing from his pores.

"No kidding," I said. "We're gonna be *right there!*"

"Somebody up there hates us." Eric pointed up at the ceiling.

"Like the universe?"

"Or the Flying Spaghetti Monster."

"You know about the Church of the Flying Spaghetti Monster?"

Eric nodded. "It's only the most awesome church in the world."

"You know what they call people who go there?"

"Pastafarians, of course."

I laughed. "I think it's actually a real church in one country, like New Zealand or something."

"Oh, I thought it was your parents' church."

"Dude, don't let my parents hear you compare Unitarians to Pastafarians."

Eric did a don't-even-worry-about-that hand flap. "I'm not scared of your parents. They *love* me."

"They don't love you enough to take us both to some other conference where Jonah Burns is autographing books."

"Wait. How do you know?" Eric grabbed his chair's armrests and dragged himself up until he was sitting straight again.

"We're not actually brothers, you know," I said, thinking about a book I'd just started about two random girls who became sisters because their parents got married to each other. "It'd be awesome, but we're not."

"I know, but, dude, we've gone on trips together before! Remember that camping trip last year?"

"You mean The Least-Fun Trip Ever Since My Dad Actually Hates Camping?"

"Well, yeah, he was super crabby the whole time, but it's totally a precedent!"

Hmmm.

"You may be onto something there, Number One." I pointed a finger at the ceiling, then dropped my whole hand until the finger was pointing at Eric.

"I think you're a little confused about who's Captain and who's Number One, but yes, yes I am."

I was getting excited. "So all we have to do is find another conference where Burns will be and talk my parents into taking us there."

"He must be doing a bunch of them, right? There are comic cons *everywhere*."

"Totally."

It turned out Jonah Burns wasn't going to a zillion different comic cons, though, because the universe is a cruel place. After almost a half hour of asking questions on SN and then digging through a bunch of websites because we didn't like the answers we got on SN, we had to face reality: the number of conventions where Burns was going to sign the *Sandpiper Iconic Edition* was . . .

"Two??" I draped my arms over my head and kicked my chair away from my desk. "He's only going to two events? Seriously?"

"Looks like it." Eric's head had been propped up on his hand, but at some point it'd slid down to his elbow, where it now lay sideways on top of his fully extended arm. "DefenderCon, and Expo Extraordinaire."

"Which is in *London*," I half barked, half laughed.

"I guess it can't hurt to ask." Eric shrugged.

"If we can go on a trip to *Europe*? What's the point?"

"Maybe your parents will be so sympathetic that they'll say yes." Eric locked eyes with me for a second, then we both snorted and shook our heads.

"You know what, I'm gonna ask just to see what they say."

"Oh, honey, that would be amazing, but there's no way," Mom said.

"I've never been to London," Dad said in a wistful voice,

which actually gave me a second of false hope, but then he sighed. "We could do it in a couple of years if we really plan for it."

"That's . . ." I groaned. I knew it was totally unrealistic for us to go on such an expensive trip—I'd looked up the airfare and practically had a heart attack when I saw how much it was—but now that we were talking about it I felt *so* frustrated. It actually made it worse that Mom and Dad were taking it kind of seriously. "That's too late. It has to be *this* year. They're not gonna do another book like the one he's signing this year."

"Matt, we just can't do it," Mom said. "You're sure this DefenderCon thing is the only other—"

"YES, I'M SURE."

I slumped over on the table and folded my hands over my head like a tent. A tent of despair.

"He's our favorite comic book artist," I mumbled. Mom and Dad exchanged one of those looks where they both make sad faces with upside-down U-shaped mouths.

"How about if we set up some other kind of trip with you and Eric?" Dad said. "We could go to some other convention that's in driving distance. Or just someplace you guys think would be fun."

"Sure, I guess," I said into the surface of the table. It helped that he wasn't being all *hey, I have a TERRIFIC idea* about it, but going to some other comic con where we couldn't get Jonah Burns to sign the *Sandpiper Iconic Edition* would be like eating a jelly doughnut that turns out to be a slice of bread wrapped around a piece of fruit leather.

"Okay," Mom said. "We'll come up with something. I know it won't be as good, though, and I'm sorry, sweetie."

"So am I," Dad said.

Mom came over and rubbed my shoulders a couple of times, then went into the living room. Dad kissed me on the back of my head and went into the kitchen, where I heard him start washing dishes.

Everything was awful.

OCTOBER MEANS HALLOWEEN, AND by the second week of the month the school was basically wallpapered with pumpkins and ghosts and stuff. Mr. D was maintaining tradition by hanging up a scarecrow he'd made himself, complete with a fake mustache that looked like his mustache. It was really good, actually—you could always tell he'd spent a bunch of time on it—and he'd always laugh when we'd tell him how much better-looking the scarecrow was than him.

I was still in a terrible mood about DefenderCon, although Scarecrow D helped a little. I tried reminding myself that at least Eric and I were still going to World of Amazement, which also kind of helped. I knew we'd eventually have to figure out who else to room with—the hotel rooms were four-person suites—but

Hector solved that problem for us, and waaaaay before it actually had to be solved.

My locker and Eric's locker were at opposite ends of the hallway leading to the music wing, and mine was at the end closest to the music rooms, so I stopped at my locker while Eric kept going toward his. Hector's locker was just a few feet away from mine, and he swung its door shut as I walked up.

"Hey, Matt," Hector said.

"What's up, Hector?" I said. It was still weird to open my locker and not immediately put my piccolo in my backpack, so I stared into it for a second before grabbing the *Giant-Size Untouchable Girl* special issue on the top shelf and stuffing it into my backpack instead.

"Not much. You picked out a Halloween costume yet?"

I shrugged. "No. How about you?"

"Yeah, I'm gonna be a zombie wrestler."

"You mean like a lucha libre zombie?"

"Yeah. You know about lucha libre, huh?"

I shook my head.

"Not really, but did you ever read that book *Niño Wrestles the World* when you were little?"

"Ooooh, right, by Yuyi Morales!" He pronounced "Yuyi"

more like "Juji," although not quite—the *J* sound was a little squishier, or something.

"Right. That's all I know about lucha libre. Anyway, that's an awesome costume."

"Thanks! So . . . you and Eric are gonna be roomies at World of Amazement, right?" Hector asked as I closed my locker.

"Yup," I said as I headed for Eric's locker. Hector's locker was even closer to the music rooms than mine, and he hustled to catch up and walk next to me. "How about you?"

"That was what I was gonna ask," Hector said with his usual super-cheerful expression. "Jack and I were wondering if you guys would room with us, like a team of four."

"What about teams of four?" Eric said, closing his locker just as we got there.

"I mean us," Hector said, spinning his index finger in a circle between us.

"That's only a team of three," Eric said.

"Us and Jack, I mean." Hector pointed past Eric and at the very end of the hallway, where a kid with brown hair and terrible posture was about to turn the corner leading to the school's front doors. "HEY, JACK, WAIT UP!"

Jack Browning played a regular old alto saxophone, but it

looked like a tuba when you saw it next to his bony torso. He was like a blade of grass with feet.

"Hey, guys," Jack said in his usual droopy-dog tone. He wasn't a sad kid, he just sounded that way. "What am I waiting up for?"

"For us, obviously!" Hector smacked Jack on the shoulder. I shouldn't have been surprised that Jack didn't stagger or anything, but he seriously looks like you could knock him over by looking at him too hard. "You got roommates for the World of Amazement trip yet?"

"Ow. No. Why?"

"Why do you think?" Hector said, grinning at me and Eric like we were in on some big secret. He was so clearly happy that I couldn't help grinning back, even as I wondered how it wasn't obvious that Hector was asking Jack to room with us.

"We need one more person for our room, Jack," I said.

"You guys know that trip's not for . . ." Jack paused and literally counted on his fingers, which was entertaining. ". . . seven months, right?"

"We know!" Hector smacked Jack on the shoulder again.

"Ow. Could you maybe not do—"

"So are you in?" Eric smacked Jack on his other shoulder.

"Ow. Will you guys stop hitting me on the shoulders if I say yes?"

We all cracked up, and instead of hitting Jack's shoulder I just put my hand on it as we started walking, and Jack ended up in the middle of our group as we all headed for the front doors.

"Dude, you actually said yes!" Hector said.

"Why do you say that, Hector?" Jack said everything so slowly that he sounded like some kind of dork cowboy, in a good way—it's like he was hilarious without actually meaning to be.

"You never say yes when I ask you to do stuff."

"Oh, that's not true—"

"Wait, how many times have you asked Jack to do stuff?" Eric said as we went through the doors and strolled down the big, wide steps in front of the school.

"Like three times!" Hector said.

"I didn't know you two were such good friends," I said.

"I don't know if my dude here thinks we are," Hector said, nudging Jack with his elbow.

"Sure we are," Jack said. "Your timing is just bad, Hector."

"Oh, it's my timing, guys." Hector looked back and forth at me and Eric, nodding his head in a fake-serious way. "That's what it is."

We stopped at the bottom of the steps where the usual post-school crowd scene was happening. Some kids were getting picked up by their parents or babysitters or whoever, but most people were either milling around and talking, or doing the smart thing and walking away from school as fast as humanly possible.

"Anyway, we're all set for the trip, then," I said.

"Yeah, thanks for making that happen waaaaay before it needed to, Hector!" Eric grinned and elbowed Hector, just to make it obvious he was joking.

"No problem! I'm taking off, roomies, later!"

"I'm going that way too, Hector," Jack said. "So long, roomies."

"I don't know, man, you sure you want to be seen with me?"

"You're pretty funny, Hector."

"We're really doing this 'roomies' thing, huh?" I said as Hector and Jack started walking away.

"We're SO doing it!" Hector said over his shoulder. He raised a fist in the air, and Eric and I laughed as we turned and went in the opposite direction.

"That was kind of cool," I said.

"Yeah, one less thing to worry about!"

We passed Summer Oh (Skye's older sister) and some girl I didn't know, who were standing and talking right at the curb.

"It's just so much pressure, you know?" Summer said, throwing her hands in the air. "How am I supposed to know what I want to study for all four years of high school before high school even starts—"

"Can't you just tell your mom you want to go to Lodestar High instead?"

"You don't know my mom—"

High school! Holy crap! I was glad I didn't have to think about high school yet, and even more glad that when the time came, I'd at least get to deal with the terrors of high school side by side with Eric. I couldn't imagine doing it without him.

RIC AND I STARTED HANGING OUT A
little more with Hector and (sometimes) Jack,
which turned out to be not bad. We even went
trick-or-treating together on Halloween, with me and Eric
dressed as Rocket Cats (the Ursu twins, to be exact), Hector as a
luchador zombie like he'd said, and Jack as a surprisingly cool
robot. So, things were going okay in November even though we
couldn't go to DefenderCon.

Then the Thanksgiving parade came along, like it always
does. It's the biggest marching band event of the year, at least
during years when we weren't going to places like World of
Amazement, and of course this year was my first time playing
bass drum during the parade, which meant I'd probably be more
sweaty than usual. Sure, the temperature starts getting down to

50 degrees by the end of November, but it doesn't matter that much when you're carrying a giant drum while wearing leather shoes, polyester pants and jacket, and a big tall hat with an even bigger feather sticking up on top. At least we didn't have to wear the hats Dad wore when he was in marching band—those things looked exactly like giant, white Q-tips. I felt embarrassed for Dad just thinking about it.

"Got all your stuff, buddy?" Dad said as we pulled up in front of school on the Saturday morning before Thanksgiving.

"Yeah. I think. It's still weird not carrying my piccolo."

"I was thinking the same thing. Looking forward to seeing you in the drum line, though!"

"Thanks, Dad."

I gave Dad an extra-tight hug, just because he was being so awesome about the drum thing even though I knew he wished I was still playing piccolo, then headed inside.

The outer doors to the music wing—which were on the same side of the school as the front doors but all the way over by the corner of the building—were propped open, so I walked in that way. The band room had that exciting, busy vibe where everyone's getting ready to perform—the equipment closets where we kept the drums, flags, and super-big instruments like the tuba were open, and people were tuning up their instruments, helping each other adjust their uniforms, and talking about whose houses they were going to for Thanksgiving (if they were going to someone else's house).

I was the first drummer to arrive, and I didn't feel like lugging my bass drum around until I had to, so I left it in the closet and waited for Eric to get there.

"Good morning, people!" Mr. D swept out of the music office with a gigantic coffee cup in his hand, surveyed the room—two-thirds of the band hadn't shown up yet, but there was still ten minutes until we were officially supposed to be there—and then swept back into the office.

I said hi to some people as they came in, tolerated Skye's frowning inspection of my uniform, and accepted a high five from Hector that almost felt mandatory because he was so enthusiastic about it.

"First parade as a drummer, huh?" he said.

"Yup. Feels weird."

"No doubt, but it's awesome." Hector did a "let's go" wave as he headed for the big equipment closets, and after another look at the door to see if Eric had just arrived, I followed him up there. We took our bass drums and mallets over to our usual seats and put them on the floor. The harnesses were basically big, padded U shapes that went over our shoulders, a straight piece of metal that rested against our chests and stomachs, and a couple of hooks to rest the drums on, so they didn't need to be adjusted or anything like that.

The room gradually filled up with people, but Eric was still nowhere to be found. Sean and Kenny walked in together, hooting and snorting about something, with their uniform jackets unbuttoned and hanging open like a couple of slobs. They clomped over to the trumpet section, sat down, and kept talking, not even pretending to get ready for the parade. Typical.

Hector made a last-minute trip to the bathroom, and as he hurried out of the band room Eric passed him on his way in. I let out a long breath of relief—he wasn't usually late to stuff—but as he walked up the steps toward me I saw his face. It looked like he'd either been crying or yelling, or both.

"You okay?" I said as he reached me. He shook his head.

"Mom got a phone call just as we were leaving the house," he said. "There's a new restaurant that just opened that only does desserts—the chef is kind of famous, and he offered her a job."

"Oh. Okay. Well, that's cool for her, I guess."

Eric snorted.

"Yeah, for her. She says it's her dream job, and a lot of pastry chefs would kill for it."

"So what's the catch . . ." I had a sudden, horrible feeling that I knew the catch.

No. Don't let it be that.

Eric took a deep breath and banged his fists down onto his knees.

"The restaurant's in New York."

No. No no no no no no.

"But that's on the other side of the country."

Eric shook his head, looking like he might cry or yell or do both again, and he furiously rubbed his eyes and nose with his forearm.

"Yeah."

"You're *moving?*"

"Not yet, but yeah."

"When??"

"Right after the last day of the school year."

No. This wasn't happening. Except it was. At the end of the school year, three weeks after the marching band competition, right after the last day of school, Eric was moving. Meaning I'd have to spend all of seventh grade, eighth grade, and high school without the best friend I'd ever had.

No.

NO!!!

EY, MATT, ARE YOU OKAY?"

I would have jumped if I wasn't wearing a huge drum on my chest, so I just twitched instead and glanced at Hector, who had a worried look on his face.

"What?"

"I don't know, man, you just look really upset." Hector was standing right next to me with a bass drum mallet in each hand. The big black feather on his hat was almost as tall as his whole head, and his green-and-black marching band uniform looked super crisp and smooth, like it'd been ironed. I looked like a wrinkled-up slob in comparison, but I didn't care. I didn't care about anything, including the parade.

"I . . . I'm . . . you know what, I'll tell you later," I said. "Fine. I'm fine."

"If you say so, dude. Come on, it's showtime."

"What's the matter, Wang?" I actually did jump when Kenny (who'd snuck up behind us) barked right in my ear. "Did you and your boyfriend have a fight?"

Sean snort-laughed as he finally appeared, with his uniform buttoned up and his bass drum on his shoulders.

"Go away, Kenny," I said in a monotone voice.

"Bro, you need to get a life," Hector said to Kenny. "Seriously."

"No, *you* need to get a life!"

"Good one, Kenny," Eric said, sounding as miserable as I felt. "So original."

"Hey, man, you better get in line before Drabek comes over here," Sean said to Kenny.

"Yeah, yeah," Kenny said, but he actually listened to Sean and left.

My favorite part of any band performance is usually when we all line up by section in the hallway leading to the back door of the school, file out into the parking lot (which is always empty on parade days), and mill around until it's time to march. The color guard is there too—they kinda feel like a totally separate thing from the band since they don't share a room with us in the building, so it makes it feel like even more of a big deal when they're out there too. Everyone's laughing and talking and nervous and scared and excited all at the same time; it's when we feel the most like an actual team, trying to do something cool together.

This time was different, though. I mean, obviously. Eric was standing next to me on my other side, just like we'd planned. It should have been awesome and fun, but Eric looked like he'd been hit over the head with a brick, and I felt like he looked.

"Okay, kids, it's showtime!" Mr. D shouted over the general chatter as he moved to the front of the band with his baton in hand. "Fall—IN!"

Everyone stopped talking and got into formation, which didn't take too long—we were mostly bunched up in our own sections already. I tried to focus on the parade instead of Eric having to move. *March. We're about to march. Get ready.*

"Marching band! Ten-HUT!"

Everyone snapped their feet together and stood up straight.

"Horns—UP!"

We raised our instruments into playing position. For us bass drummers that just meant raising our mallets to the middle of our drums, ready to thump out quarter notes.

"Mark time, mark! And—one! Two! Three, and four!"

We started marching in place, keeping an eye on Mr. D as he waved his baton in time, but it was really hard to concentrate—I started a beat late and stepped with my left foot when everyone was already stepping with their right, so I had to stand on one foot for a beat to get in sync, and then I almost missed it when Mr. D said "forward—MARCH," and almost quick-stepped to catch up even though I didn't actually miss it.

We marched across the parking lot and around the school building. The starting line for the Thanksgiving parade was about six blocks away from the school, in front of the fire station, and people were already starting to bunch up on the sidewalks by the time we arrived.

"Prepare to halt!" Mr. D said as we got closer and closer to the other groups who'd already gathered. "And—BAND, HALT!"

"One, two!" everyone shouted, stomping our right feet down on "one," and our left feet down next to them on "two." A bunch of people started clapping and cheering, and I felt suddenly mad at them, which didn't make any sense, but nothing was making sense anyway.

"At ease," Mr. D said. "Stay in formation, though—we tune up in five minutes, and the parade starts in ten."

Everyone lowered their instruments, slouched out of attention and into normal standing-around positions, and started talking. Not me and Eric, though. We looked at each other, and I wanted to talk to him about him moving, but I also didn't want to talk about it because I didn't want it to be true. I couldn't think of what to say or how to say it, anyway, and Eric must have felt the same, because we just stood there and stared at the tops of our drums without saying anything.

It was unprecedented in the history of us being best friends, and it was horrible. Thanksgiving, ha. Eric was going to move, and it was already messing things up. I didn't feel like giving thanks at all.

"HAPPY THANKSGIVING!" someone in the back of the crowd shouted. Of course.

"Easy——" I had to stop and clear my throat, since I'd been fighting off tears since we'd started marching back at the school. "Easy for you to say."

I didn't speak loudly enough for whoever that person in the crowd was to hear me, but Eric snorted, and it sounded so much like a normal, nonsilent, Eric-style snort that my heart went *zing!* in my chest.

"Yeah, happy Thanks-for-nothing-giving," he said in a croaky voice, which was when I realized he'd been crying too.

Mom and Dad like to say how it's okay to cry, crying is healthy, boys need to cry too, blah blah blah, but they don't understand how *dangerous* it is to cry in front of other kids, especially other boys, and there were a lot of kids from school in the crowd, so Eric and I tried to make it look like we were coughing and shielding our eyes from the sun instead of clearing our throats and wiping our eyes. Even that was better than not talking to each other at all, though.

"Band! Ten-HUT!"

Everyone had stayed in line, so we all snapped to attention fast.

"Mark time, MARK! And one, two, three, and four . . ."

We started marching in place, and Eric and the other snare drummers set the beat by hitting their drumsticks together, *click, click, click*, and *click*. We were right behind a bunch of fancy cars full of important old people like the chief of police and the city council, and we heard their engines starting up for a second before the crowd drowned them out by clapping and cheering. I risked putting one mallet-holding hand on Eric's shoulder for just a second, and he looked sideways at me and nodded his head in an "I'm okay" kind of way, but I knew it wasn't true. He wasn't okay, and neither was I.

"Band! Forward, MARCH!"

The show had to go on, though, and as the parade started moving for real, I felt a gloomy relief about playing the bass drum instead of the piccolo, because another lump had formed in my throat, and I was pretty sure I wouldn't have been able to play a single note.

HANKSGIVING FELT AS THANKLESS
as I thought it would, and December wasn't much
better. I usually like December—there are Christmas presents and two weeks of no school to look forward to,
and Eric's mom usually makes a bunch of amazing desserts—
but the news that Eric had to move was like a fog of awfulness
hanging over everything. It was also hard to eat those amazing
desserts without thinking about how they were kind of the reason
Eric's mom was making them move away. I ate them anyway—
they were still really good—but I wasn't, like, 100 percent happy
about it.

It didn't even help when the holiday break started, because
Eric's grandmother lived in the same area they were moving to,

and his mom decided they'd spend the entire vacation visiting her. We wouldn't get to hang out during the holidays at all.

Mom, Dad, and I went to the Cedarville Unitarian Universalist Church when we still lived in Cedarville—I still kind of miss it, even though some of the sermons were really boring. Mom and Dad are always all worked up about politics and stuff like that, so it was the perfect church for them. After we moved, they dragged me along to two other Unitarian churches, a Zen meditation center, and an Episcopalian church that supposedly had a really good choir, but they said none of them felt right, so we ended up going back to the Cedarville church for Christmas and not going to church at all the rest of the year.

So there we were, going to the Christmas service like usual, driving through a horrible traffic jam in downtown Cedarville.

"Wow, this is . . . ," Mom said.

"Yeah," Dad said, drumming his fingers on the steering wheel as we stopped behind a car that was so shiny and new, it practically glowed in the dark. "And it's only been two and half years since we moved."

"That's new, isn't it?" Mom pointed at a building on the opposite side of the street. The words "Yoga Magic" were painted sideways on one wall in huge letters, big enough to go all the way to the roof. The whole front window of the place was filled by a picture of a skinny blond woman in exercise clothes, palms pressed together in front of her like she was praying, and sitting in that hard crisscross-applesauce way where your feet are on top of your legs.

"Yup," Dad said.

"Ugh."

"On the bright side, the schools are still terrible, so our reason for moving is still valid!"

Mom sighed. "Double ugh."

"It's very endearing when you say 'double ugh,'" Dad said, leaning over and kissing Mom on the temple. She leaned into it. Triple ugh.

"Why do we keep coming back here if you guys hate it so much?" I said as we drove on—slowly—through the neighborhood.

"We don't hate it," Mom said.

"Sure we do," Dad said.

"'Hate' is a very strong word, honey."

"Yeah, Dad," I said. "Stop hating, start participating."

Dad snort-laughed. "Where'd you get that phrase from?"

"From you."

It was Mom's turn to laugh.

"Hey, look!" Dad pointed at a car that was pulling out of a parking spot half a block ahead of us. "Parking spot! Miraculous! IT'S A MIRACLE!"

"Hands on the wheel, Miracle Man," Mom said as we pulled into the spot.

"What's that?" I said, pointing at the store we'd just parked in front of. Dad looked.

"That, my son, appears to be a store that sells dog leashes. And nothing else."

People wearing heavy coats and lots of red or green clothes were heading for the church, which looked mostly the same to me—same location on the corner; same big, pointy roof; same stained glass doors. We walked up the front steps and joined the line of people at the doors. Mom and Dad waved and said hello to a few people, but I kept my mouth shut and just waited in line.

"Hello, Park family!" Reverend Cinnamon waved at us from the chapel entrance as we walked through the front doors. One time I heard a couple of old men at the church making fun of her name, and it made me so mad because Reverend Cinnamon is always nice and never makes fun of anybody. People are terrible, and mean people are extra terrible. "So nice to see you again!"

"Hi, Cinnamon!" Mom and Dad said at the same time.

"Happy holidays, Matt!" Reverend Cinnamon gave me a little wave, and I smiled back.

Mom and Dad have said we used to sit all the way in the front when we still lived in Cedarville, but now when we come back for the Christmas service we sit all the way in the back, which was fine with me. Just being there was weird; sitting in the front row would probably make me feel like a zoo animal—trapped, with nowhere to hide. We found three seats on the aisle, all the way in the corner of the chapel.

"—focusing on voter suppression, it's so obvious—"

"—it's typical trans-exclusive radical feminist nonsense—"

"—that *Oregon Trail* game totally erases Native genocide, don't—"

At home, Mom and Dad were the only adults I ever heard talking about stuff like trans-exclusive radical feminists and Native genocide. At this church, *every* adult talked about that kind of stuff.

Eventually everyone settled down and the service began. Reverend Cinnamon gave a quick sermon about the usual stuff—staying grounded during times of commercialism, how Jesus was a brown-skinned Middle Eastern refugee, etc. and so on—followed by the Christmas pageant, which ironically had some family's white, blue-eyed baby in the role of baby Jesus, but whatever. I liked the part where we sang carols, especially "Silent Night," when everyone lit candles and the chapel lights were turned off.

After the lights came back up everyone either milled around, hugging and talking, or headed for the chapel doors to say hi to Reverend Cinnamon, making a gigantic, sloppy, terrifying line. Mom and Dad were talking to a friend of theirs whose name I couldn't remember, so I put my hand on Mom's elbow and waited. She's said a million times that when I do that she'll definitely ask me what I need as soon as she's done saying whatever she's saying, but the actual success rate is probably about 66 percent.

"Hi, sweetie, what is it?"

Success! I like it when Mom calls me "sweetie," but it always feels a little dangerous. It's kind of like saying "you may now punch my son in the face."

"I'm going to get cookies, okay?"

"Okay!" Mom turned back to what's-her-name, and I headed for the side door of the chapel, which led to a hallway that went along the back of the church where the classrooms and stuff were.

It was the long way around, but it was almost deserted. I saw a group of kids walking ahead of me, and as the chapel door closed behind me they burst out laughing and kind of crashed into each other, shoulders rubbing and heads leaning toward the middle of the group. They disappeared around a corner, and being in the empty hallway suddenly felt like being on the surface of the moon. By myself. After the planet Earth had just exploded.

I took a deep breath and kept going. Luckily I made it into the meeting hall when it was still mostly empty. There was a stage at one end of the hall and a kitchen at the other end, with two long tables full of cookies right in the middle. The kids I'd seen in the hallway were already there, along with a couple of others—six or seven kids in all. As I walked up to the table they looked at me for a second, and most of them went right back to looking at the cookies, but a couple of them smiled and *then* went back to the cookies, which I guess was something.

I took my time looking at all the cookies—at this church you never know how many will be made with stuff like coconut flour or chopped dates—and then looked for a place to sit. More and more people were coming in, but I saw a corner of the meeting hall that still had a couple of empty chairs in it, so I hurried over there.

I took a chomp out of an oatmeal raisin cookie as two of the kids I'd seen in the hallway started talking about some kind of trip they were taking in super-excited voices.

"What did your dad say about sharing the house?"

"He's still thinking about it—he says there's not enough privacy when we all stay in the same house."

"He says that every year, though."

"Yeah. He'll probably say it next year too, and we'll probably stay in the same house again anyway."

"My mom says it's way cheaper."

"It's more fun when we can all walk down to the beach together."

"Well, except for my brother. He hates walking."

"Your brother hates everything."

"True . . ."

Is this what it'll be like when Eric moves away?

Eric and I weren't going on any trips with our families. The marching band trip was going to be awesome, but the whole band would be there, including the evil people in the band. It wouldn't be just *us*.

I was mad at the two kids talking about *their* trip practically right in front of me, even though I knew it was totally unfair to them. I was mad at Mom and Dad for saying we couldn't go to Expo Extraordinaire just because it was in London, I was mad at Jonah Burns for only showing up at two conferences in the entire *world*, and I was mad at World of Amazement for scheduling its Spring Festival at the same time as one of those two conferences, because right after it was over Eric would be gone.

I wish we could meet Jonah Burns before Eric moves.

The band trip is as close as we'll get.

We'll never get a better chance . . . to . . .

. . . a chance . . .

I swallowed a mouthful of cookie, stuffed the rest of the cookie I was holding into my mouth all at once, and realized Eric and I *could* take one last trip together. A really short one, too: about three miles, round trip.

I reached into my jacket pocket and dug out the crumpled sheet of paper I'd been carrying around to torture myself with, smoothed it out, and looked at the words spelled out in big, red letters at the top:

DefenderCon Schedule

"**AIT, LET'S DO WHAT?**"

"Let's go to DefenderCon."

Eric stared at me with his mouth literally hanging open. I cackled.

"You look like a cartoon character with your mouth like that. All that's missing is the tongue hanging out."

We were in one of the music wing's small practice rooms, which had the benefit of being soundproofed so nobody could listen in on our conversation. I had my flute, and Eric was just sitting in a chair. He was in the corner that you couldn't see from the little window in the door, though, and since it was still the first week of January (which meant it was still the first week of orchestra instead of marching band) we were probably safe for the whole half hour between the end of the school day and the start of practice.

"What are you talking about?" Eric said. "We can't go to DefenderCon!"

"Yes, we can."

"How??"

"We can walk—I mapped it. They're not much more than a mile apart."

"Dude, you know what I mean."

"Yeah, I know, but look at this. I'm gonna—" I saw somebody walk past the window of the practice room, so I handed Eric two sheets of paper with one hand and lifted my flute with the other. Eric looked back over his shoulder just as someone else actually stopped to look in, probably checking to see if the room was occupied.

"Yeah, practice a little, we gotta make it look good."

I played the first thing that popped into my head, which was the new Alex Gino song, "Kitten Time." I wasn't very good at it, but it worked—the face disappeared from the window as I fumbled through the melody and Eric looked at the papers.

One of the papers was the World of Amazement Spring

Festival schedule Mr. D had handed out before the holiday break, and the other was the DefenderCon schedule. I'd done some strategic highlighting on both, and as Eric looked at them I played a few warm-up exercises. It was kind of shocking how rusty I felt after not playing either piccolo or flute for six months—my cheeks started feeling tired after playing *one* arpeggio in C, for example, and I sounded super wispy. I felt a little embarrassed when I finished and looked at Eric, but he wasn't paying attention to my flute playing at all.

"So let me get this straight." Eric had one schedule in each hand, and he waved them around for emphasis. "Jonah Burns will be at DefenderCon on the last day of our World of Amazement trip."

"Yes."

"You know we have to do marching band stuff the whole time, including the last day."

"Yes, but—"

"But the last day is . . ." Eric looked briefly at the paper in his left hand. ". . . 'Have Fun at World of Amazement Day,' which is—"

"—*the day after the Spring Festival!* Meaning it's not really a *marching band* day!"

I lifted my flute and played a short trill for dramatic effect. It sounded good too.

"No, but we'll still be there with the rest of the band. The teachers are probably gonna do check-ins and stuff."

"No doubt, but think about it—if we're going on rides and checking out the gift shops and stuff, there's no way the teachers can keep track of everyone at every second—"

There was a flash of motion in the window, so I quickly played a few notes from a Tchaikovsky solo I'd played last year ("Dance of the Flowers," I think) just to maintain our cover.

"That makes sense." Eric dropped his hands onto his knees and was staring off into space, which meant he was picturing the scene in his head. "Nobody's gonna want to go all on the same rides all at the same time. So . . ."

"So there should be windows of time when we can sneak out and get back without anyone noticing!" I raised a fist in the air.

"You're hilarious," Eric said. "Is that like a dork power salute?"

"Yes. Obviously."

"Super-dork powers, activate!" Eric raised his fist too, dropping one of the schedules in the process.

"For the honor of Dorkskull!" I pumped my already-raised fist.

THE **BOYS** IN THE **BACK ROW**

"Seriously, though, this is a pretty risky plan." Eric reached down and picked up the schedule off the floor, then handed them both back to me. "We could totally get kicked out of the Spring Festival."

"Forget that, we could get *expelled*." I didn't really want to think about that too hard, but it was too obvious to ignore.

"Yeah. That would be bad."

"So . . . what do you think?" I looked Eric in the eye and fiddled with the keys on my flute. "Is it, you know, a good plan?"

"It's an AWESOME plan!" Eric smiled, and this time it wasn't a scary-clown grin—it was a real, this-is-the-best-thing-ever smile, and I relaxed. "It's risky, sure, but . . ."

"But it's, like . . ." I took a deep breath. "Our only chance to, you know . . ."

Eric's smile faded a little. "Yeah. I know."

"I mean, we're not going to London for Expo Extraordinaire."

Or anywhere else.

"We *have* to do it," Eric said, sounding like he had something stuck in his throat, then coughing into his hand.

"Yeah." I said, suddenly feeling super determined, which was way better than feeling sad. "I mean, think about it. It could be legendary."

"It means playing hooky, basically."

"It means *breaking a lot of rules.*"

"Dude, you're hilarious," Eric said with a grin, sounding like his usual self again.

"What?"

"You can't WAIT to break so many rules all at the same time."

"I have no idea what you're talking about."

"It's obvious."

"No it isn't."

"You might as well hold up a sign that says 'law-breaking nerd' or something." Eric did a wiping motion with one hand, palm facing me.

"I'm the biggest law-*abiding* nerd in the whole school! Do you actually know me at all?"

"Everybody knows that, but I'm the only one who knows you also have this hidden troublemaker thing going on—I mean, come on, look at this bananapants plan you just came up with."

"Welp, sometimes the operation of the machine is so odious and makes you so sick that you just can't do it anymore. Or something."

"Ha!" Eric sat up as straight as he could and pointed at me, all dramatic and stuff. "Proof! I have no idea what it is you just said, but it's totally proof!"

"It's by Mario somebody. Mom has a mug with that quote on it."

"You're a total rebel, Matt." Eric was grinning so hard I could see his gums. "I see you."

"Dude, that grin is terrifying. You look like a homicidal clown."

"Seriously, though, we could get in super-serious trouble," Eric said. "No, actually not. I'm moving to another state, so they can't really do anything to me, but YOU could really get in trouble."

"Dude, who cares? This is, like, our grand finale, right? How cool would it be?"

"Really, really cool."

We had to take a minute to just sit and think about it, because ghosting the entire band and going on a secret expedition in a strange city without permission was next-level stuff. It could be legendary, and having a legendary stunt under my belt would be good for next year. It'd help keep my mind off the fact that Eric would be on the other side of the country.

I took a deep breath and blew it out with a long *hooooooooo* sound, and Eric nodded without saying anything. Then we both practically jumped through the roof as someone knocked really hard on the practice room window. Skye Oh was glaring at me through the glass, and she jerked her thumb in the direction of the band room while mouthing the words "let's go!"

I nodded and started taking my flute apart, while Eric looked over his shoulder at Skye and waved. She waved back, but also did one more very emphatic thumb-point toward the band room before disappearing from view.

"Has Skye always been this bossy?" Eric said as he stood up.

"Yeah, but she's always right too."

"She never does that to me." Eric made a fake sad face.

"It's probably an Asian thing," I said. "She acts like I'm her little brother or something."

"Huh. How much older is she?"

"*I'm* two months older than *her*. Summer does it too, but at least she actually is older than me."

I finished packing up my flute and stood up, intending to stuff the printed schedules into my back pocket, but instead I held up the DefenderCon schedule so we could both look at it. I looked at Eric and did a big, theatrical gulp that wasn't totally fake. He broke out the scary-clown grin, but he also grabbed my shoulder and shook it, and when we left the practice room he put an arm around my shoulders and shook my whole upper body hard, and I smiled broadly enough that I probably looked like a scary clown too.

KYE EYEBALLED ME AND ERIC LIKE
an old Korean auntie as we walked into orchestra
practice, which she'd been doing since the fourth
grade, not long after Eric and I became best friends. It started when
I made the mistake of telling Mom and Dad there were three other
Korean American kids in the band. They were so excited to know
there were other Asian people in town that they called Skye's parents and invited the whole family over for dinner without even asking me. I mean, seriously! Stuff like that should be illegal!

I felt a little bit excited about it too, though, at least after I
stopped being mad about the not-asking-me thing. I really
thought I'd become friends at least with Skye, and maybe Summer and Graysin too. It was fourth grade, you know? I was more
optimistic back then. This is how it actually went down.

"Hello!"

"Welcome!"

"So nice to meet you!"

"Thank you for having us!"

Adults always say the exact same things to each other when they go to someone else's home for the first time. Mom always says "welcome!" to guests like she's happier than she's ever been in her whole life. Summer and Skye both said "hi, Matt," while Graysin just said "hey" and waved. He smiled in a way that was cool and collected but also legitimately friendly, and I instantly liked him.

"Nice to see you outside of school," Summer said, nudging me on the shoulder, then walking past me into the living room.

"Thanks," I said with a big smile.

"Hey, don't get too excited," Skye said, giving me more of a punch on the shoulder. "It's not like we don't see each other practically every day already."

I laughed. There was a lot of shuffling around, shoes being taken off, jackets being thrown on the futon in Mom and Dad's office, and "I love your house" and "oh, it's such a mess" kind of comments by the parental units. Mr. and Mrs. Oh turned out to be super nice, which was a relief—I mean, you never know about other kids' parents—so it felt like a good start, at least until we all sat down for dinner, where Summer and Skye spent the whole time talking to . . . my parents. Mostly my mom.

"Here's what I think," Skye said, waving a carrot stuck on a fork in the air for emphasis.

"Look out, Skye's thinking." Graysin ducked his head when Skye waved a fist in his direction.

"Hey, hey, watch it with the hands," Mr. Oh said.

"Yeah, and how about eating that instead of using it like a sword?" Mrs. Oh said.

"I think the person who's the doctor should have their name listed first, the end." Skye nodded her head like she was agreeing with herself, then took a triumphant bite of carrot.

"You're such a child," Summer said. "That's not the point."

"Well, it should be, and you're a child too, you know."

"You know what, it's not a bad point," Mom said, passing the saltshaker to Dad. "Getting that 'Dr.' in front of your name takes a lot of work, and if that's the reason one person's name is first on the envelope, it should be the reason for everyone, including women."

"And *girls*," Skye said, raising an index finger above her head.

"And girls," Mom said, laughing along with the other adults. Summer didn't laugh, though.

"But that's *my* point," she said. "What if two people are married and they're both doctors? Who comes first then? And what if they're nonbinary?"

"What if they're both nonbinary?" I said. "I'm just say—"

"Here's what *I* think," Summer said, like I wasn't even there. "The woman's name should always come first, even if it ends up like 'Mrs. and Dr. Lee' or something like that. It's been the other way for too long."

"It's like evening the historical scales," Mrs. Oh said.

"Also a good point!" Mom looked like she was having the time of her life. "Just because something's always been a tradition doesn't mean it has to stay that way."

"Unless it's a good tradition—" Skye said.

"Yeah, like—" I tried to jump in, but Skye just kept on going.

"—though I guess it depends on *who* thinks it's a good tradition."

"Uh-huh—"

I definitely wasn't used to being interrupted so much at dinner, and it must have shown on my face, because Graysin caught my eye and leaned in my direction.

"You get used to it," he said.

"You guys doing okay over there?" Dad said with a grin.

"Yeah, no side conversations," Skye said, hinting at future bossiness to come.

"What does that even mean, 'no side conversations'?" Graysin said.

"Lot of interrupting going on," I said to Dad. He shrugged.

"It's okay."

Which I guess it was, but as Dad turned to say something to Mrs. Oh, Mr. Oh told Skye and Graysin to stop arguing, and Mom and Summer got into what looked like a very intense conversation between just the two of them, I wondered what Eric was doing, and how soon I could get Mom and Dad to invite *his* family over for dinner.

It'd be nice to say that was all ancient history, but dinner with the Ohs became a once-a-year-or-so thing at our house, and each time Skye sank her teeth a little deeper into the bossy sister role. I still liked Skye, and in a way it was nice to know she cared, but if I had to pick between fantasy siblings, Eric would win in a landslide. Besides, planning for Operation Get Jonah Burns's Autograph required serious planning in the present. We even decided to do some of it at school, during lunch, as a fun way to kick off February.

We'd printed out a new copy of the DefenderCon schedule,

plus copies of the conference center map, and maps of the neigh-
borhoods around World of Amazement and the conference
center. Then we plotted out how to get there from World of
Amazement, which turned out to be exactly 0.68 miles away. We
didn't bring all that stuff to school, of course—that was just asking for trouble. Bringing *any* of it to school was asking for trouble,
which we were forced to remember the hard way.

"Piece of cake," Eric said. He pinned the printed-out neighborhood map onto the cafeteria table between us and took a bite
of his sandwich that was in his other hand. "That's a third of the
way from here to Hero Worship."

"Yeah, but that's not the part that worries me," I said, eyeballing Eric's bag of potato chips. The open end of the bag was
turned toward Eric, meaning it was turned in the wrong direction. "We can walk to Hero Worship and buy comics without
having to sneak out. We need a way to get out of the amusement
park without being seen."

It was simple, actually. The first day of the trip we'd mostly be
on the bus (which could either be fun or a total nightmare), and
when we got there we'd check into the hotel and have dinner
with all the other middle-school marching bands. The second
day we'd practice in the morning, have lunch, and do the actual

competition part. The third day we'd be at World of Amazement. Going on rides, playing games, checking out the gift shops, and eating candy.

For the whole day.

"This is awesome, isn't it? It feels like, I don't know, an adventure or something." Eric took his finger off the map, then used it to turn the potato chip bag around and push it toward me. I took a few out, being careful not to break the big ones left in the bag.

"Yeah, if you define 'adventure' as 'the possibility of being grounded for life.'" I took one of the two peanut butter cups I'd snuck into my lunch box and tossed it onto the map, where it sat for two or three nanoseconds before Eric scooped it up. "But yeah, it totally is."

"Sometimes the risk of being grounded for life is what makes life worth living," he said, holding a finger up into the air, then cramming the whole peanut butter cup into his mouth at once.

"Dude. That is profound."

"Yup." Eric smacked his lips. "I'm a deep thinker."

"I was being ironic."

"I know. I wasn't. Embrace the risk, Matt!"

"Are you kidding? *I play a girl's instrument*—that's, like, the riskiest thing a person can do at our school."

Eric grinned, then poured the potato chip dust at the bottom of the chip bag straight into his mouth.

"Okay then, Captain Risktaker, when's the best time to do it?" he said, spraying a few chip fragments out of his mouth.

"We can't do it at lunchtime," I said.

"Definitely not," Eric said, nodding. "Everyone's sitting and eating."

"High surveillance."

"We need *chaos.*"

"Maybe we should just get it out of the way and take off right after we get there," I said. "Everyone's gonna be super excited, running around . . ."

"Yeah, but you know what the teachers are like at the start of a field trip," Eric said, pointing first at his own eyeballs, then at me.

"True. End of the day's not gonna work either."

"Nope."

"Right after lunch would be perfect," I said. "If you look at the World of Amazement map, the food court is really close to the entrance."

Eric chewed on his thumbnail as he thought about it.

"Huh. That could work."

"Yup." I started to get that feeling when something's coming together, like playing a note-perfect piccolo solo during an assembly, or looking at a picture of Cloudsplitter and knowing I got every angle of his helmet exactly right. "And all the kids will scatter again, but the teachers'll be less on it, you know?"

"That doesn't give us a whole lot of time to get to Defender-Con, though," Eric said. "Remember the schedule? The Jonah Burns signing is at one thirty."

"I know, but I think we can make it. There's a bus that leaves from the main WoA entrance right around one and gets to the conference center in about ten minutes."

"It takes *ten minutes* to go less than a mile? That's bananas," Eric said. "We could walk there faster . . . Wait, that's your point, isn't it?"

I nodded my head, feeling smug, and Eric laughed.

Somebody said "queers!" in a loud voice on the far side of the cafeteria, and we instinctively froze and looked around without moving our heads too much—whipping your head around to see which nerd exterminator shouted "queers" isn't a winning strategy—but nobody seemed to be sending their orc soldiers to our table, so we relaxed.

"Okay, right after lunch. Do we need some kind of—"

"Dudes, what's up?"

It was Hector. For once he didn't have his usual super-toothy grin in place, maybe because he was too busy frowning at the other side of the room. Someone gave a harsh seal-bark of laughter, and someone else (I mean, pick a bully, they're everywhere) said "sit down, Carlos!"

"My name's not Carlos!" Hector shouted. Of course that's when Vice Principal Falano decided to pass by the cafeteria doors, and because our usual table is close to both the bathrooms and the doors (making a fast escape is super important for bathrooms and cafeterias), Falano heard Hector shout. He stopped, pivoted, took one step through the cafeteria doors, and pointed at Hector.

"You. Come with me."

"What? Why??" Hector said.

The laughter from the other side of the room was muffled, but still harsh.

"Don't make it worse," Falano said, still pointing.

Hector leaned back and turned his face to the ceiling, knees bent and arms flopping. I heard him mutter something, but his lips were mashed together so I couldn't hear exactly what.

"I want to talk to you guys," he said to me and Eric as he stood up straight again. "About drummer stuff."

"Totally," I said.

"Dude, so unfair," Eric said in a low voice.

"Welcome to my life," Hector said.

"Mr. Morales. NOW."

"Yes, sir." Hector walked out after Mr. Falano with his head up and his fists clenched.

The cafeteria was mostly quiet while that was all going on, but when the door closed behind Falano every person in the room started talking at once.

"What do you think he means, 'drummer stuff'?" Eric said.

"Beats me. I guess we'll find out, unless Falano has him expelled or something."

The bell rang, and the already super-loud noise level went through the roof. We usually had our stuff ready to go before the bell rang, but the Hector Saga totally distracted us, and of course the map showing the route from WoA to DefenderCon was still on the table, just waiting for Kenny Delacroix to run over and grab it. Which he did, of course.

"Hey, losers, is this yours?" he said. Sean, who was trailing behind Kenny like a loyal sidekick, snorted and laughed.

"OH, COME ON!" I said. I lunged across the table to try to take it back, but Kenny gave my shoulder a fast, hard push, and

I had to grab the edge of the table to keep from falling off as he took a closer look at the map.

"What is your problem??" Eric said, but Kenny just ignored him.

"Dude, what've you got?" Sean asked as he walked up to the table. He put a hand on Kenny's shoulder, and Kenny shook it off.

"It's a World of Amazement map, see," Kenny said, pointing at the big, gray rectangle labeled "World of Amazement" that filled up one whole corner of the page. Kenny and Sean looked at each other and shook their heads as if carrying around a map was a horribly tragic thing to do.

A map of the neighborhood around World of Amazement isn't the same as a map of World of Amazement, I thought.

"Can I see?" Sean asked, reaching for the map.

"NO!" I said. "Give it back!"

Sean and Kenny looked at me with straight faces, then looked at each other and cracked up.

"A map," Kenny snorted, still giggling like a serial killer. "What a couple of dorks." With two quick motions he tore the map into pieces and sprinted for the cafeteria doors, throwing the pieces into the air as he ran. Eric and I gave each other a tired look. Replacing the map would be easy, but it was the principle of the thing, you know?

Sean looked at us and shrugged as he slowly started walking after Kenny. I glared at him for a second, then turned my back on him.

"Why does Kenny do stuff like that?" I asked. Eric shrugged.

"Why do dogs eat their own vomit?"

I couldn't help laughing. "What the heck are you talking about?"

"You haven't heard that before? It's in the Bible."

"I'm Unitarian, you know, we don't read the Bible."

Eric snorted. "I forgot. It's totally in there, though—'a dog returns to its vomit,' or something like that."

"Why are you so weird?"

"I don't know!" Eric said. "Why are you best friends with someone so weird?"

"I don't know either, but let's go."

I didn't want to be late to class—I never want to be late to anything—and everyone was following Kenny out of the cafeteria, so we stood up and slung our bags over our shoulders. There didn't seem to be much point in looking for the pieces of the map now that everyone was walking right through the place where

Kenny dropped them, and when I saw Sean up ahead of us looking at a scrap of paper in his hand, I wondered why he hadn't run to catch up with Kenny like he usually did.

I didn't even think about what he was looking at, and I definitely didn't remember that I'd written "DefenderCon" right there on the map in big, black letters.

13

THE THING WITH KENNY AND THE MAP was a big downer, even with jokes about dogs eating vomit, and the rest of the day wasn't a whole lot better, maybe because it was February and everyone was getting crabby that it wasn't spring yet. By the time the last bell rang, Eric and I were both in serious need of cheering up.

"You know what we need after a day like that?" Eric said as I shut my locker and shrugged into my jacket. It took me a second to get it, but when I did, we looked each other in the eye and said it at the same time:

"HERO WORSHIP!"

It was a long walk in the depressingly cold weather from school to Hero Worship, but it was worth it, because Hero Worship is the best comic book store in town. The surprising thing is that it's not the only comic book store in town. Not that I hate Paradigm Shift—we go in there every once in a while just to check out what kind of weird new toys they have in stock—but they're all about independent publishers and stuff that's mostly about regular people, and mostly adult regular people. They don't carry *any* superhero comics, so there would have been no point in asking the first question we asked when we got to Hero Worship.

"Do you have the new Sandpiper omnibus?"

The girl with the BAMF! tattoo who was working the front counter laughed, throwing her head back. It was a friendly sounding laugh, though, and she'd always been nice to Eric and me, so I didn't mind.

"I guess that's a no, huh?" Eric said, leaning forward with both hands on the comic shop counter. A pile of stickers that said "Keep Reading Comics" tipped over and spilled between his hands, but Tattoo Girl scooped them up in one deft motion and put them back in a pile on the counter in front of me. We knew the answer was gonna be no, but why not ask anyway? Miracles happen, right?

"I'm sorry, guys, but no, we don't," she said with a shake of her head. The single lock of green in her otherwise brown hair fell over one eye, and she tucked it back behind one ear. "That book is super limited edition. It's not even being sold in stores. Your best bet is probably DefenderCon."

"We're going to DefenderCon!" Eric and I said at the same time, like a couple of dorks.

Tattoo Girl smiled big, showing all her teeth. She had an amazing smile. "You guys are so cute," she said.

"Er . . . thanks?" Eric said.

"That's really cool that you're going to DefenderCon! How'd you talk your parents into it?" Tattoo Girl said.

"Uh, our parents are pretty cool about stuff like that," I said, trying to sound casual.

"That is awesome," Tattoo Girl said, crossing her arms and nodding slowly. "My folks would never have driven that far just to take me to a con. You guys are gonna have the best time."

"Have you been to DefenderCon?" I asked.

"Yeah, a couple of times. It's cool. It's not anything like the really big conventions, but that's probably okay for you guys, being first-timers."

"Oh," I said. Tattoo Girl was making it sound unimpressive, and it must have shown on my face because she held up her hands, palms facing me.

"Dudes, the smaller cons aren't bad," she said. "I like the big cons because I get to see a lot of friends, and they have tons of swag, but I was totally overwhelmed by the first one I went to. It was huge, you know?"

We didn't, but she was making sense. We were gonna be there by ourselves, after all.

"Got any advice for a couple of first-timers like us?" Eric said.

"Sure." Tattoo Girl held up an index finger. "One, don't be a creep. I mean, I've seen you guys in here a lot, so I know you're not creeps, but there might be guys and girls in costume, and sometimes the cosplayers show a lot of skin. Don't stare— staring's creepy."

Guys and girls?

"Two." She held up another finger. "There's a lot of free stuff, but don't grab everything. Posters are cool, but they're hard to transport. Buttons are also cool, but they take up more room than you might think they do. T-shirts are good because you can wear them, stickers are good, comics are the best."

Eric and I grinned at each other, geeking out at the thought of all that free stuff. Tattoo Girl looked toward the back of the store, also grinning, and I saw one of the other store clerks grinning back at her.

"You guys are so cute!" Tattoo Girl said again. She held up her hand with her index finger, middle finger, and thumb all sticking out. "Okay, three. Don't take any crap from other attendees—the comic book world is still kind of backward in some ways. There are a lot of *other* creeps. Got it?"

We nodded, and Tattoo Girl folded up her index finger and middle finger and stuck out her thumb.

"Thanks," I said.

"No worries. We do have the new issue of *Dimensional Nexus*, if you guys want to check that out. Sandpiper's in it."

"Totally!" Spoken in unison again, but whatever.

Tattoo Girl pointed at the wall on the opposite side of the store from the registers, but we already knew that was where the new releases were. I followed Eric around the display of bobble-heads and plush toys in the middle of the floor, and we found the new *Dimensional Nexus* after a minute of browsing the shelves.

"So that was cool," I said. "Weird, but cool."

"Yeah, I guess."

Eric carefully flipped through the first few pages of the new *Dimensional Nexus*. I leaned in to look, close enough that my shoulder smushed up against Eric's. A second later I heard what sounded like the word "adorable" from behind us, so I peeked over my shoulder. Tattoo Girl and the other clerk, a taller girl with a T-shirt that said "BE KIND" in flowing, scripty letters, and "UN" right before "KIND" in bright red, blocky, slightly diagonal letters, like it'd been stamped there. They stood behind the counter with their arms slung over each other's shoulders, both grinning openly at us.

I smiled weakly back.

"They're looking at us," I mumbled out of the side of my mouth into Eric's ear.

"Who?" Eric looked around, almost whacking me in the face with the back of his head. When he made eye contact with the girls they laughed and split apart, and Unkind Girl (who actually seemed kind enough) went back to the other end of the store, still chuckling.

"Dude, whatever, who cares? I'm getting this." Eric carefully closed the issue of *Dimensional Nexus*, I grabbed one for myself, and we took them to the counter.

"Why do you call us 'cute' all the time?" I blurted out. Tattoo Girl lifted an eyebrow, still smiling as she rang up the comic for Eric.

"Oh, come on, I don't say that all the time."

"Okay, no, but you've said stuff like it a few times," Eric jumped in. "What's up with that?"

Tattoo Girl slid the comic into a bag, handed it to Eric along with his change, then leaned on the counter with both arms.

"All right, since we're getting real here, my name's Gabi." Tattooed Gabi stuck her hand directly at me. I held out my hand, and she grabbed it, pumped it once, and let go.

"I'm Matt."

"Good to meet you. And you?" Gabi's hand swiveled to Eric, who also had his hand grabbed and shaken.

"Eric."

"That's Angie back there," Gabi said, pointing with her thumb at the back of the store, where Angie was waving her arms around while talking to a guy in a hoodie with an Atomic Aardvark plush toy in his hand. "We were just saying how great it is that a couple of young dudes like you are so, you know, comfortable being together."

Eric and I looked at each other, then back at Gabi.

"Especially around here, you know? I mean, it's not the worst place in the world, but people in this town can be pretty backward about that stuff," Gabi said.

"About what stuff?" I said, honestly curious. "Being best friends?"

"No, I mean, you know, being together."

Oh. That again.

Eric blew out a long, gusty breath, looked at the ceiling, and shook his hands like a mad scientist saying "it's alive!" I leaned away from the counter and slapped myself on the forehead, and we slumped into each other like a couple of zombies, shoulder to shoulder.

"Wow, that's quite a display, guys," Gabi said. "Very theatrical."

I put my elbow on the counter, planted my forehead on the palm of that hand, and looked up at Gabi by rolling my eyes up until I could see her.

"We're not, you know. Boyfriends."

"Yeah, I got that." Gabi tilted her head and gave us a sideways smile that was small, but also very nice, maybe just because her whole face looked relaxed or something. "It's okay, you know."

"So . . . why did you think we're gay?" Eric said.

"Do you guys think there's something wrong with being queer?" Gabi crossed her arms and squinted at us, suddenly looking a lot less relaxed.

"No, of course not!" I said.

"You sure?" Gabi said, slowly raising one eyebrow.

"Yes! We just . . . we're not gay, or queer, you know? Why does everyone think we are?"

"Not everyone's as nice about it as you," Eric said. Gabi snorted.

"Oh, you guys have NO idea," she said. "Okay, well. I think it's mostly because you guys are just sweet with each other, you know?"

"Sweet how?" I said.

"It's not like we make out with each other," Eric said.

"No, that's not what I mean," Gabi said. "Look at that thing you did before, with the"—she made claws out of her hands and shook them in the air like Eric had—"and the leaning together and stuff. You guys touch each other, you know? Not in a creepy way, just in a way most guys don't."

"That's it?" I said. "Because we touch each other?"

"Mostly that."

Eric and I looked at each other, but looked back at Gabi when she burst out laughing.

"It's the way you do that too! You guys look right into each other's eyes!"

"So what?" I said. "Other guys look each other in the face too, don't they?"

"Not that long, and not without making stupid bro jokes," Gabi said. "You guys just look at each other without even talking."

Eric and I looked at each other again.

"Dude, it's kind of weird to look at you now," he said.

"I know, right?"

"Sorry, I didn't mean to make things weird," Gabi said, grinning.

I sighed. "It's okay, I guess."

"It gets a lot worse than this," Eric said.

"I believe it." Gabi shook her head. "People suck. I think you guys are awesome, for what it's worth. Got it?"

"Got it," we said together.

Gabi grinned. "Awesome. Let me ring that up for you, Matt."

As she dug my change out of the register I heard someone line up behind us. I looked over my shoulder out of pure reflex, and my eyes almost fell out of my head when I saw the shocked-looking face staring back at me. It was Sean. I mean, of *course* it was Sean. Life would have been simpler if it'd been just some random kid we don't know.

"Hey, look at you coming back so soon! Nice!"

I spun back the other way to look at Gabi, who was looking past me with a one-sided smile. I looked behind me again, but there wasn't anyone else back there. The only person she could have been smiling at was Sean, who was holding a copy of . . .

The Rocket Cats Ultimate Collection.

Geez, what *was* going on? It was cool to meet another fan, or would have been, except it was Sean, so we weren't actually meeting him because we already knew him, and if it was someone we actually were just meeting, we wouldn't know what they're like, but we already knew what Sean was like. Sean was like . . . himself. He was so *Sean.*

"Thanks, guys," Gabi said. I was so busy whipping my head back and forth that I moved my hand just as she was putting my change into it. The clatter and ping of money hitting the floor felt really loud. I crouched to pick it up.

"I see you guys know each other." I could only hear Gabi from down there on the floor, but her voice sounded amused and curious.

"Yeah, we know each other," Eric said, eyeballing Sean with what I call his "isn't *this* interesting" face as I stood up.

"We go to the same school," Sean said, using a voice that was almost like his normal one, except less stuck-up than usual. He looked the same as usual, though—still taller and skinnier than me, and still blonder than Eric. He paused, almost like he was making up his mind about something, then went on. "What's up, guys?"

"Hey, Sean," I said out of sheer reflex. What color was the sky in this world?

"I was kind of hoping to run into you guys here."

What? Why?? Because you took our DefenderCon schedule at school and now you want to talk about DefenderCon?

Nothing good could happen if we talked about Defender-Con. We had to avoid the subject no matter what.

"Well, we got all the Rocket Cat fans in the world right here," Gabi said. Eric and I stepped aside as she held a hand out to Sean, palm up. He handed *The Rocket Cats Ultimate Collection* to Gabi and dug a black leather wallet out of his back pocket.

"You guys probably have one of these already, huh?" Sean said as Gabi rang him up.

"He does," Eric said, pointing at me with a thumb.

"Cool."

"Do you guys know there's gonna be a Rocket Cats TV show?" Gabi said as she gave Sean his change.

All three of us started talking at once.

"Yeah, it looks *amazing*—"

"It's on Crusader Central, so it won't be for little kids—"

"It's the same people who did *Metalcore Raccoon Lodge*. That was awesome—"

We stopped all at once when we realized what was happening: Eric, Sean, and I were all talking about *Rocket Cats* together in a totally psyched, non-suspicious (for me and Eric), non-jerkface (for Sean) way. Like we were, you know, friends.

We must have all gotten weirded out at once, because we all stopped talking and started staring at each other at the same time.

"Here."

We looked at Gabi, who had a big grin on her face and was holding some kind of postcard in Sean's direction. He took it from her and looked at it, and I got a good look at the side facing me before he flipped it over. It had a red background with one word on it in white letters with black outlines: DEFENDERCON.

Welp. There went our chances of avoiding the subject.

I looked at Eric, who looked back at me, but then I noticed Sean was looking at Eric, and suddenly Sean and I were looking at each other (which was uncomfortable and weird), then Sean and Eric were looking at each other (which I didn't like *at all*), then we were all kind of looking back and forth between each other (which was even more uncomfortable), and finally we all just looked down at our feet because what the heck was even happening??

We were rescued by the sound of a very loud person coming into the store. The little bell hanging by the front door jingled violently as a tall, bushy-haired guy in a black T-shirt with nothing but the Blue Beetle logo on it—*awesome* shirt—came inside. He was obviously a friend of Gabi's, because he stepped up to the counter right next to Sean and stuck a handful of what looked like tickets right into Gabi's face.

"GABRIELA!" he bellowed. "BEHOLD!"

"Can't," Gabi said. "There's a giant, sweaty hand in front of my face."

She was laughing at the same time, though, and as she pulled Blue Beetle Guy's hand away from her face she put her other hand on his chest. Her eyes opened wide as she looked at the slips of paper in his hand, then she let out a "WHOOP" and thrust her arms in the air.

"YEAH! How'd you get these??"

"By hunching over my laptop and hitting the refresh button for hours and hours. TicketWizard is . . . less than wizardly."

"Well, yeah, but how was it not sold out?" Gabi was hopping up and down, she was so excited. She'd completely forgotten we were even there, so Eric and I seized the opportunity to head for the door and leave as quickly as possible. Of course it wasn't quiet because of the stupid bell over the door, but we made it out onto the sidewalk, and as we started walking I felt a wave of relief at leaving all that strangeness behind us. It was a lot colder outside of the store, but also a lot less weird.

It didn't last long, though. We'd only gotten as far as Bunduck Hardware, the hilariously named store two doors down, when the door to Hero Worship jingled again.

"Hey . . ."

Eric and I stopped and looked at each other with our "I have a bad feeling about this" looks on our faces. Then we sloooowly turned around to look at Sean, because of course Sean had followed us out of the store. The fact that we just had the most awkward trip to Hero Worship ever didn't mean things had to stop getting more awkward, right?

Sean was carrying a brown paper bag with his new Rocket Cats book in it in one hand. It couldn't have been anything else, and of course Sean would hide the book inside a paper bag like that. Eric and I got harassed a lot, but it didn't stop us from actually being ourselves. Well, most of the time, anyway. A gust of cold wind hit the display in front of Bunduck Hardware, rattling a stand of Christmas lights with a "75% OFF!" sign on it, and I stuck my hand that wasn't proudly holding my new copy of *Dimensional Nexus* into my jacket pocket.

"I have a bad feeling about this," Eric whispered as Sean

walked up to us looking . . . hesitant? *Nervous?* He looked nervous. Maybe it was because he was wearing a puffy blue coat—it was harder to look cool in a winter coat. I felt nervous too, which just made this Day of Unexpectedly Having Things in Common with Sean McKenna weirder. Was it ever going to stop?

"Are you guys thinking about this?" Sean held up the postcard and pointed at the big "DefenderCon" on it.

"Thought about it how?" Eric said.

"Thought about whether you're going or not, doofus," Sean said. "Doofus" sounded a lot less mean in his nervous voice, to be honest, but come on. Mean is mean.

"We've thought about it," I said, feeling annoyed.

"Seriously?" Sean said, dropping his hands and flicking the postcard onto the sidewalk. Another blast of wind briefly lifted it off the sidewalk, and it settled a few feet farther down the block.

"Can you not do that?" I said.

"Dude, it's fine," Sean said, not even looking at the postcard. "Whatever. You said—"

"What Matt *meant* was yeah, we've thought about it, but we don't want to get expelled," Eric quickly jumped in.

"Uh, yeah, I mean, DefenderCon would be super cool, but it's during the band competition," I said.

"Well, actually it's on the day after the competition," Sean said. "You know, the optional day."

The *optional* day? What kind of menace to society calls the last day of an out-of-town field trip "optional"?

"It's the World of Amazement day," Eric said. "Do you seriously want to skip out on the rides and stuff?"

"Yeah," Sean said, sounding like his usual, irritatingly confident self. "Meeting Jonah Burns AND sneaking out right under Drabek's nose at the same time? It'd be legendary!"

I couldn't stand it anymore, and I silently raged at my parents for not letting me have a phone, because I totally would have faked a phone call from them just to get away from Sean.

BZZZZZT.

Eric's phone was vibrating! It was a Christmas miracle! It was six weeks late, but whatever!

Eric fished the phone out of his pocket, tapped it with a thumb, and held it up to his ear.

"Hi, Mom. Yeah, we're coming." Pause. "Now? Do we have to . . . okay, okay. Bye."

Eric stuck his phone back into his pocket and waved at me. "We gotta go, Matt."

"Now?" I had no idea what he was talking about, but I knew it was fake and I should play along.

"Mom got the time wrong. We need to hurry." Ah, the old "Mom messed up the restaurant reservation" scenario. Eric was already walking away, fast. "Bye, Sean."

"Hold on, can you guys just—" Sean said, but I was already running after Eric.

"Sorry, Eric's mom will kill us if we're not on time!" I said over my shoulder. "See you later!"

Sean said something else, but we were too busy running down the block, around the corner, and to the end of downtown where the big "Welcome to Hilltop Summit" sign was (yes, our town's name is two words that basically mean the same thing) to hear. We ran across the street, where we finally flopped onto the bench outside of the laundromat, flapping our coats open and shut to cool down without getting actually cold. Mrs. Nee, the owner, peeked out of the laundromat door and waved, and we waved back. Sean's house was in the opposite direction, so hopefully he wasn't following us, but we only sat there long enough to catch our breath, then started walking to Eric's house, since we'd been about to go there anyway.

"So that wasn't actually your mom, was it?"

"Nope." Eric stuck out his chest. "I set the alarm clock on my phone in the store just in case something like that happened."

"Dude, you're awesome!" Everyone should have a best friend who doesn't trust the people who can't be trusted as accurately as Eric, am I right?

"So, wow, that was different," Eric said, zipping his jacket back up as we walked. The sun was just starting to dip behind the trees, and it was getting seriously cold.

"WHAT THE WHAT WAS THAT . . ." I flailed my arms in the air, then let them drop.

"What do you mean, what the what was whatever it was you just said?"

"I mean, what does this *mean*?"

"What do you mean, what does it mean?"

"DUDE. STOP. I just don't like not understanding reality anymore."

"Yeah, well, reality didn't make a lot of sense before, Matt."

"I have the most bizarre thought, and you're gonna laugh at me, but I'm telling you anyway."

"Oh, come on, when have I ever laughed at you?"

I snorted. "Dude. That makes ME want to laugh. At you."

"Seriously, I won't laugh." Eric stood up really straight and did a big cross-your-heart motion with one index finger.

"I had a thought about Sean, like we could be, you know, friends, if things were different. As if all Rocket Cats fans could potentially be friends, right?"

"Right." Eric kept his promise. That's the great thing about Eric—I can trust him to take stuff seriously when I need him to.

"And Sean's not, like, pure evil all the time like Kenny."

"I guess," Eric said. "He's a little evil, though."

"Well, yeah, but just a little."

"And they're really good friends, so it's not like pure evil *bothers* Sean."

"I guess that's true."

Eric nodded. "When I saw him with the Rocket Cats book, I wondered if he was trying to set some kind of trap for us. Is that bad?"

"I don't know if it's bad. Might be a little paranoid, though, since he's never actually done that."

"Maybe he's just been pretending to not be evil all along, dun dun duuuuhhhhh!" Eric raised his arm and made a few up-and-down stabbing motions.

"Okay, that actually is paranoid. Like, super paranoid."

"I know." Eric started drumming his fingertips on his knees. "I think if somebody had stepped on a butterfly five years ago, it would have altered the space-time continuum, and Sean and I might be friends today. We're not, though."

"True. Also, the butterfly effect might have ended up with you and me not being friends."

Eric snapped his fingers and pointed at me. "Exactly! Or you and Sean might be the ones who are friends today!"

"Which would be *terrible*," I said.

"No it wouldn't, you'd be friends! It'd be normal!"

"Now I can't even remember why we started this conversation . . ."

"Everything's normal, in other words?" Eric grinned.

"Oh, har dee har har," I said. "I guess what I mean is . . . what if we could be friends with Sean now?"

Eric shrugged. "Could we? I mean, sure, he likes the Rocket Cats, but does that automatically mean we like him now?"

"I guess not."

"Yeah. I don't know about you, but people who call us 'queers' and 'boyfriends' as much as Sean does aren't exactly the people I want to go to DefenderCon with."

"Yeah, I guess not. Which means we have to figure out what to tell him."

"Why do we have to tell him anything?" Eric said.

"Because he clearly wants to go to DefenderCon with us, don't you think?"

Eric shrugged. "I mean, yeah, but so what? He doesn't know anything for sure."

"It's gonna be pretty obvious when we're *not* at World of Amazement on the last day."

"Who says?" Eric said as we turned the corner onto his block. "Everyone will be doing different rides and stuff—that's the only thing that'll make it possible to go. We'll just make sure Sean doesn't see us leave, and then it won't matter if he wanted to go with us or not."

"Maybe."

I couldn't help thinking it was more complicated than that, though.

IT WAS ANOTHER FEW WEEKS BEFORE
we found out how serious Sean was about going to
DefenderCon with us, partly because Eric got the flu and
missed a whole week of school, and partly because I tried really,
really hard to avoid Sean. Lucky for us I had a lot of practice
from dodging bullies, or maybe I should say unlucky for us. It
also helped that I was in the flute section for orchestra, which
meant Sean and I were basically at opposite ends of the room. He
pounced on the very first day Eric was back at school, though.
He didn't actually come talk to us until practice was over and
everyone was on their way home, when we thought maybe we'd
escaped for another day.

The weather was nice too—it was sunny, the sky was bright
blue, and only two or three fat, puffy white clouds were floating

around up there. It was like the universe was getting ready to pull the rug out from under us. We'd just gotten over all the stress of listening to other kids brag about how many valentines they got on Valentine's Day while we didn't get any, but did Sean care? Noooooooo.

"Hey! You guys!"

At first I didn't even recognize the voice coming from behind us as we walked up the big hill that started on the block right next to school, mostly because it sounded more friendly than snarky. It was only when we turned around and looked that I realized it was Sean.

"Oh hey, it's Sean," Eric said in the kind of voice you might use to say "I have detention for the next three weeks."

"Methinks he wants to parley," I said, wondering if it would be too suspicious to just take off running and try to lose Sean by cutting through people's yards.

"Dude, you know you can't pull off that epic fantasy warrior voice."

"Who died and made you the elven king?"

"Hey," Sean said again as he stopped maybe seven or eight feet away. It was a weirdly in-between distance—not really next to us, but not *not* next to us either. Most kids at school who lived in the same direction as us took the long way home because the hill is so steep, which was why Eric and I always walked up the hill. Fewer hassles, you know. So the three of us had the hill's three blocks of sidewalk all to ourselves, with the houses on either side of the street looking ominously quiet and empty. There were cars in some of the driveways, but still. It was finally getting close to spring, but the vibe of the whole situation was almost Halloweenish, like there should be gray skies and dead leaves blowing in the wind. Now it felt wrong that it was sunny and too warm for winter jackets.

"I wanted to give this back to you guys," Sean said, holding out a piece of paper. It was crisscrossed with tape on the back. "Sorry about that."

Sorry about that? Was Sean *apologizing* for something? I reached out, took the taped-up piece of paper, and held it so Eric could look at it too. It was the map Kenny had ripped to pieces— Sean must have picked them up and taped them back together. The "DefenderCon" written on it was ridiculously clear. I had no idea why we thought it'd be a good idea to bring it to school.

Eric and I looked at each other, and I tried to tell him to be on guard by subtly wiggling my eyebrow. I wasn't sure if it worked, though.

"Er . . . thanks?"

"Did you look at it?" Eric said, suspicion dripping from every word.

"Of course," Sean said, like it was no big deal to read someone else's private stuff.

"So . . . why are you giving it back?" I said, feeling cautious.

"Wow, guys, paranoid much?" Sean held up his hands, palms facing us.

"Yes," Eric and I said in unison.

"So you remember what we talked about a couple weeks ago? At Hero Worship?"

"Wait, was that you?" Eric said, rubbing his chin.

"You're not fooling anyone, Costa," Sean said. "Are you guys seriously gonna bail on the last day of the trip to go to DefenderCon?"

And there it was, our big secret plan just thrown right out there on the sidewalk.

"No," Eric said.

"Yeah," I said at the exact same moment. Eric slapped his forehead, then turned to give me a look of death. I gave him a slumped-shoulders, "I'm sorry" kind of shrug. Sean gave us a sideways grin.

"You guys need to work on getting your story straight," he said.

"DUDE," Eric said, ignoring Sean and staring at me with his hand still clamped to his forehead. Eric can pack a lot of communication into a single "dude," like *what are you doing, I thought we were on the same page here*, and *we are not going to Defender-Con with Sean!*

"Hey, it's not like we talked about this."

"Well, yeah, that's true. You could have just, you know, gone with it."

"Dude, seriously, I just can't."

"What, can you not tell a lie or something?" Sean said with a smirk.

"No," I said.

"He's just *really bad at it*," Eric said, talking to Sean, but looking at me.

"Are you like some real-life version of Mr. Fearless?"

Eric and I turned our faces toward Sean super fast—if someone was drawing a picture of us, we'd both have swoopy motion lines to show how fast our heads turned. Mr. Fearless was a Golden Age superhero, originally created more than a hundred years ago. He was super strong, impervious to metal weapons, invulnerable to radiation, and was considered kind of a dork for his "I never tell a lie" policy. His comic ran for about a hundred issues, but he'd never been on TV, in a movie, or retconned to have a secret, traumatic origin story, so the only people who knew about him were hard-core comic readers and collectors.

"Lying's too much work," I said. "And you know who Mr. Fearless is??"

Sean pulled a pack of gum out of his pocket, slowly unwrapped a piece, stuck it in his mouth, and nodded once as he put the pack back in his pocket without offering us any.

"So . . . you read comics besides *Rocket Cats*," Eric said. Sean gave another solitary nod, slowly chewing his piece of private gum the whole time.

It wasn't just the comic books that was bizarre—lots of kids at school read comics; it's not like Eric and I were THAT unusual—but the whole "talking to us about it while being an obnoxious jerk for only part of the time" thing? For the *second* time? INCREDIBLY bizarre.

"Huh. That's . . . cool," I said.

"Yeah, maybe. Or not." Eric was unconvinced, which was probably good. It's important to keep one person on mental guard duty. Still, I was wondering if this was a chance to get

Sean to stop being obnoxious all the time. Mom and Dad like to talk about "the interconnected web of human existence" and "finding meaningful commonalities"—it's a Unitarian thing—and what's more webby and meaningful than comic books?

I wasn't exactly anxiety-free, though. It's not like we were talking to Summer Oh, who treats us like people worth talking to even though she's older than us and thinks comic books are ridiculous and is almost as bossy as her younger sister. This was still Sean.

"You mentioned Jonah Burns when we were at Hero Worship, but do you know who he actually is?" Eric said suddenly, crossing his arms and using a keep-'em-off-balance kind of interrogation method.

Sean crossed his arms too, and he somehow managed to lean backward while he was still standing up.

"Yeah," he said, drawing it out so long that it sounded more like "eeeeeeyeeeaaaahhh."

"What's his best series?" Eric said, not messing around at all.

"Duh, Atomic Aardvark."

Eric and I shared a fast, sideways "huh" look. Atomic Aardvark *was* good.

"What do you think of Sandpiper?" I said, because while I liked Atomic Aardvark too, Sandpiper is the greatest.

"Aw, Sandpiper sucks," Sean said, waving his hand like he was blowing away the smell of a fart or something. "Burns is terrible at drawing chick heroes."

I blinked. *Chick heroes?*

"Did he really just say 'chick heroes'?" I said to Eric in a "wait, what?" kind of voice.

"Sandpiper doesn't show any skin," Sean said. "She doesn't have a boob window; she wears pants instead of shorts or skirts. I mean, come on, why bother drawing her at all?"

Yeesh. Everything about that explanation was gross.

"You know that's totally sexist, right?" I said, immediately feeling like a dork as I said it. Mom and Dad have told me a million times how awesome it is to just come right out and say stuff like that, but I still felt like a dork saying it. The first time I said it at this school was in the cafeteria on my first day, and being laughed at, punched on the shoulder, and harassed for the rest of the day by the biggest, meanest guys in the whole school isn't the kind of thing I get over super fast.

"Oh, give me a break, Park," Sean said.

"Yeah, Park," Eric said, sticking his lower jaw way out like a bulldog. "Give the big strong man a break."

Sean opened his mouth, looking ready to throw down in a bigger way, but he paused, stuck his hands out like Captain Stupendous stopping a runaway train, and gave his head a quick, sharp twist to the side. The crack from his neck was totally audible, ech.

"Wow," Eric said, sounding honestly impressed by the loudness of the neck crack.

"You know what, I'm not talking to you guys just to harass you," Sean said, putting his hands into his back pockets and doing his leaning-backward-while-standing thing again.

"Could have fooled me," Eric said.

"Haha," Sean said.

"Yeah, about that," I said. "Why *are* you talking to us?"

We all knew why—Sean wanted to go to DefenderCon with us, it couldn't have been more obvious—but I was starting to feel mad about it. This was supposed to be *our* final adventure, just me and Eric. Sean could speak for himself!

"Your plan to go to DefenderCon is awesome, and I want in."

GAH. Why did Sean have to go and speak for himself?

W**E STOOD THERE AND STARED**
at each other for a minute, and I mean a
solid sixty seconds all in a row. SUPER
awkward.

"For real, huh," Eric said, making it sound not even a little bit
like an actual question.

"For real," Sean said. "It'd be cool, right?"

The thought that jumped into my head just then took me
completely by surprise.

It could be.

Being suspicious of people all the time is an incredible bum-
mer. You have to keep your guard up whenever you're around
those people, you can't trust what they say even if they're not
always trying to mess with you, and you have to watch what you

say because you never know if it'll be used against you. And the thing with Sean is he doesn't always try to mess with us—unlike Kenny Delacroix, Sean can actually seem like a not-terrible person. He does mess with us sometimes, though, so it's not like he was suspicion-free. That was when the huge, crackling lightning bolt of guilt went through me.

Me and Eric. Me and Eric. NOT me, Eric, and Sean.

I'd actually been thinking about going to DefenderCon with Eric *and Sean!* And it wasn't about Sean, it was about me and Eric!

"Why aren't you going with Kenny?" I said.

Sean shrugged.

"Kenny's my best bud, but he's not into comics."

"Too bad," Eric said. "You guys could have started a fire in the hotel or something as a distraction. That'd be a hundred percent Kenny."

"Nah, he's not into it. Besides, it'd definitely be cool for you guys if I went with you. Like, awesomely cool."

"Awesomely cool," Eric said in his most deadpan, monotone voice.

"Did you actually just say that?" I said.

"Oh sure, Matt, it's not every day we get to hang out with,

you know, the guy we stand next to in band practice every day at school."

"Hey, hey, I'm just kidding," Sean said. "I mean, this would be different from band—you guys would get to hang out with me—but it'd all be undercover, so no one would know anyway."

"Because it'd be so embarrassing for you, huh?" I said.

"Dude, no, because we don't want to get caught."

"Oh, you're right, we didn't even think about that," Eric said, splaying his hands over his cheeks like the screaming person in that painting of a screaming person.

"Anyway, you don't have to decide right now," Sean said, sounding like he was doing us a giant favor. "Just think about it."

And just like that he turned and walked down the hill, brushing at his hair with one hand before sticking it back into his pocket. A car passed him on its way up the hill, then passed us, doing that Doppler effect thing where the sound of its engine gets higher as it gets closer, then drops as it gets farther away. We stared after him until he reached the corner at the bottom of the hill, crossed the street, and disappeared behind the house on the *other* corner at the bottom of the hill.

"Welp, we can't say that was a surprise," Eric said.

"No, but it might have been the most confusing moment of my entire life," I said.

"Yeah. It's kind of . . . too bad, you know? That he can't go with us," Eric said, and whoosh, the relief! It wasn't just me. There are *reasons* Eric and I are best friends, and one of them is the way we both torture ourselves with guilt.

"Yeah, it really is too bad."

"This is our thing, though. He can't go," Eric said firmly, and I nodded.

"He's not gonna like it," I said.

Eric snorted. "You think?"

Reverend Cinnamon used to talk about not doing things just to make people stop being mad at you, but I still hated it when people got mad at me, even when it was mean people. And now I was getting mad at myself for hating it when people get mad at me.

"Don't tell me you're worried about Sean getting mad," Eric said. "You're not, are you?"

"No," I lied.

"Liar."

"Okay, *yes*. What if he tells Mr. D?"

"What if he does?" Eric said with a shrug.

"Well, you know, there's that whole getting-expelled-from-school thing."

Eric sighed. "We can't get in trouble for something we haven't actually done yet."

"That's my point—if the teachers know about it, they'll be watching for it. It would end up being something we didn't do! Or did do? Wait, now I'm confused . . ."

"GAH," Eric said, slapping his forehead. "So . . . we need to change the plan."

"How?" I threw my hands up in the air. "We're gonna get the time of the Burns thing changed? I don't think so."

"You know what we need to do is calm the heck down and think this through somewhere that's not, you know, this hill." Eric pointed at the house we were standing in front of.

"Yeah, it's HQ time."

"Fortress of solitude" time means going home by ourselves, and "HQ time" means going to either of our houses together, and we headed to my house just because it was closer. We made a quick stop for fuel—some people call it "junk food"—but we were settled in front of my computer before too long. Mom was at work and Dad was out grocery shopping, so we didn't even have to feel guilty about bringing junk food into the house like usual.

"So our biggest problem is—" I began.

"—that you picked the worst possible time to tell Sean the truth about something," Eric finished.

"Yeah, I . . . wait, the *worst possible*? That is so cold."

"The truth is a dish best served cold. Or something."

"That's revenge, genius."

"Whatever, Matt, you're just so . . . so . . . honest."

"What, you want me to be less honest?" I said with my most fake-surprised look.

"YES. Be less honest."

"Why don't *you* be less honest?"

Eric cackled. "Didn't you spontaneously decide all by yourself that we need to be *more* honest?"

"My point is, your plan to just lie and tell Sean we chickened out and we're not doing it would be too much work. We'd have to maintain the lie for *months*."

"Piece of cake," Eric said, still chuckling.

"Only if it's, like, a dog turd cake."

"Gross." Eric opened a bag of potato chips, took out a handful, and handed me the bag.

"ANYWAY," I said through a mouthful of chips, "we can't change the time of the Burns signing, although I guess we could leave earlier."

Eric shook his head. "We'd have to leave too early, and who knows what could happen—what if Sean just watches us every second and tells Mr. D as soon as he notices we're gone? They'd send a flippin' search party after us before we reach the sidewalk."

"And if we leave too late we'll definitely miss the signing," I said with a groan.

Me and Eric. NOT me, Eric, and Sean.

"So I guess we have to, what, negotiate?" Eric said.

"Nope. I have a different idea."

"Are we gonna beat him up?" Eric said in his most serious voice, and we stared at each other for a few seconds before bursting into laughter.

"Ah, that's a good one," I said.

"So spill it." Eric crossed his arms and raised his eyebrows at me.

"You might not like it."

"Only one way to find out."

"Let's just . . . tell him the truth."

Eric sat there silently, then blinked hard.

"Wait, that's it? Tell him the truth that we don't want him to go with us?"

"Well, I was thinking more like tell him that it's, you know, a really big deal for me and you."

I looked down and started fiddling with the now-empty potato chip bag in my hands.

"It is, you know," I said in a quieter voice, "a really, really big deal."

"Yeah, I know."

"Maybe Sean will get it." *I hope, I hope, I hope.* "He kind of went out on a limb asking to go to DefenderCon with us, don't you think? Maybe he'll understand."

I looked up at Eric, and he spread his hands open in a who-knows gesture.

"I guess. So it'll be like . . . appealing to his better nature, huh?"

I nodded.

Eric cracked a grin. "You sure he actually has one?"

I gave out a soft poof of laughter. "No, but let's find out."

E DECIDED TO GO TO SEAN'S
house right after figuring out our strategy,
no advance notice or anything. We were
hoping the element of surprise would work in our favor. Or
maybe we were just impatient.

Sean's house looked a lot like all the other houses on that
block—two stories, white with blue trim, perfectly oval bushes
on either side of the front walkway, and a lawn so bright green
that it probably glowed in the dark. There was a huge jade plant
covered with tiny white flowers growing in a giant pot next to
the front steps. We'd biked past the house a million times—it
was only six blocks from Eric's house—but we'd never had a reason (or an invitation) to go inside.

"You ready?" Eric said as we stood at the bottom of the steps, looking up at the front door. I took a deep breath.

"Yeah. We're all clear on the plan, right?"

"Yup." Eric took a deep breath of his own.

"We're just gonna tell him the truth and hope he—"

"—doesn't make a joke about us being boyfriends or something, because seriously—"

"It's gonna be totally fine!"

Eric gave me a slow, droopy-eyelid kind of look.

"Excellent timing on the sarcastic look, but it's gonna be fine!"

"I'm not so sure."

"All right, fine, I'm not either, but it's the only plan we've got," I said. I tried to loosen up by hunching and dropping my shoulders a couple of times. "Let's do it."

We took the steps two at a time, and I pressed the doorbell with my thumb. A series of five chiming notes rang out inside the house. A few seconds later Sean's mom opened the door. I assumed it was his mom, anyway—neither of us had ever met her.

"Can I help you?" she said in a voice that sounded both cheerful and fake. An alpha-mom voice, as my parents would say.

"Hi, is Sean here?" Eric said, bringing his own fake-cheerful-voice A game.

Sean's mom looked surprised, which was both interesting and mysterious.

"Yes, he's here."

She had a bundle of papers in one hand and a book tucked into the armpit of the arm she was holding the door open with. She propped the door open with her foot, stuffed the book more deeply into her armpit, and stuck the papers up in there too. It was kind of impressive, to be honest. She stuck the free hand in my direction, fake-looking smile still in place, and I took it, partly to keep myself from stepping backward and falling down the steps.

"Hi. Christine McKenna."

"I'm Matthew."

She pumped my hand twice, then went through the same routine with Eric.

Sean's Mom Christine McKenna had long, very shiny brown hair, extremely white teeth, and blue eyes that made me uncomfortable with how intense they were. Being looked at by Sean's mom made me feel kind of like a zoo animal.

"Nice to meet you. Sean doesn't have friends come by very much—did you two lose a bet or something?"

She winked to show us she was kidding, but geez, what a crappy thing to say about your own kid. It was also weird because Sean still wasn't really having friends come by.

"What about his band?" I said without thinking.

Sean's mom crinkled up her eyebrows.

"Band?"

Whoa. Did she not know what I was talking about?

Had Sean been lying about his band all along??

"Marching band, we just need to talk about marching band stuff," Eric said, smoothly covering up the fact that I was just staring at Sean's mom, probably with my mouth hanging open.

"Ah, of course, marching band stuff. Come in, Sean's in the boy cave."

"Is that like a small man cave?" Eric said. She pressed an index finger against the side of her nose, then pointed it at Eric as we stopped at the foot of a staircase.

"My husband would say the only thing missing in Sean's boy cave is a girl, or maybe two girls," Sean's mom said. "You boys know what it's like to hear things like that, though."

Well, no. If Dad said something like that I'm pretty sure he'd walk up to Mom and *ask* her to rain fire down on him.

"Yeah," Eric said, surprising the crap out of me. I mouthed "really?" at him, and he nodded with a straight-lipped expression.

"Boys will be boys, even when they're grown men in their fifties," Sean's mom said with a laugh. She was seriously one of the weirdest people I'd ever met.

"Hey, I recognize that shirt!"

She was looking at my Rocket Cats shirt, which I'd just revealed by unzipping my hoodie.

"That is so *cute!* It's a good thing Frank's out of town, though. He'd probably have a stroke with two of those in the house at once. It's bad enough that Sean sleeps in his."

Wow, Sean wore a Rocket Cats shirt to bed. He was a legit superfan, just like me. Not even Eric was that much of a fan. It was starting to feel like everything I knew about reality was wrong.

"MOM."

Oh hey, it was Cave Boy himself coming down the stairs, looking at his mom with murder in his eyes. His face looked like a series of V shapes, with his eyebrows, eyes, and nose pointing down, and his mouth pointing up.

"What are you DOING, Mom??" Sean growled. Dude, so disrespectful.

"Hi, sweetie—oh right, you don't like being called sweetie anymore." I guess Sean's mom didn't mind being growled at.

"That's because I'm not five years old."

"I know, you're a very large man. You and your dad, I swear. Look, it's a unicorn!"

She held her hand out toward Eric and me like we'd just been unveiled or something. I stopped wondering if she could get any more strange and started wondering if she could *stop* getting more strange.

"You know, visitors? So rare!"

Sean just glared at her, his face turning red.

Wow. I actually felt bad for Sean, which is also as rare as a unicorn.

"Oh, toughen up, buttercup, I'm just having a little fun with you. Look, your friend has the same kitten shirt as you, it's cute."

Sean looked horrified, then started sputtering in rage.

"I don't—he's not—"

I wanted to say *ARGH, THEY'RE NOT KITTENS*, but picking sides in a fight between Sean and his mom was an obvious no-win situation, so I kept my mouth shut.

"I'm getting back to work, sweetie," Sean's mom said, totally ignoring his sputtering rage. "You and your friends have fun."

She turned and walked away from the stairs without even looking at Sean again. He tensed up, almost like he was gonna leap off the stairs and kick his mom or something, but instead he took a deep breath, looked at us, and did a "come with me" reverse head nod.

"Do you really sleep in a Rocket Cats shirt?" I said to Sean's back. No answer.

"I mean, I think that's cool," I said, but again, no answer.

Sean's room was all the way at the end of a hallway, past a bathroom and a window that looked out on a yard. He trudged up to the door, pushed it open with the heel of his palm, and walked in, holding the door open for us behind him. We followed him through the door. It felt a tiny bit like entering a supervillain's secret headquarters.

Sean's room had the same vibe as Sean himself—kind of cool, but also kind of show-offy and impersonal. The walls were the same pale yellow color as the walls in the rest of the house, but they were covered with posters for bizarrely named bands I'd never heard of. One said "Melancholy Sasquatch," with an illustration of a tambourine next to a big, muddy footprint. Another was a poster for something called "The Shoutycaps War"—all in caps, of course—and a third said "Erin Murphy's Dog: Live at Big Sky."

"Have a seat," Sean said, sounding annoyed and welcoming at the same time. He went over to his desk, pulled out the swivel chair that was pushed under it, sat down in it himself, and waved vaguely around at the rest of the room. Eric and I sat on the bed.

"Sorry about my mom." Sean said it in a voice that was pretty close to his usual I'm-too-cool-to-be-seen-around-you way, but it sounded just a little bit forced. Unusual.

"No worries," I said.

"She's the worst," Sean said, making me feel like I hadn't said anything at all.

We were in dangerous waters. Sean's mom really was kind of mean—seriously, who makes fun of their own kid—and we wanted to stay on Sean's good side, but the rule is you don't talk trash about someone's mom. That's, like, universal.

"Yeah, well, moms gonna mom," Eric said in a super-cheerful voice. Sean made a *huff* sound that was either an angry laugh or just angry.

"Anyway, so what if you have a Rocket Cats shirt?"

"I don't have a *shirt*," Sean said, snarling a little bit. "I mean, yeah, sure, I did when I was a little kid, but that was a long time ago. Why would I have one now?"

I, the kid who wears his Rocket Cats shirt to school on a regular basis and was actually wearing it right there in front of Sean, gave him my best dead-eyed, zombie-faced look, and he immediately straightened up in his chair and reached his hands out in my direction, fingers spread and palms facing me.

"Dude, it's totally cool that you wear yours! It's just, you know, people at school care how I look. You don't have to worry about that stuff."

Just when you think it can't get any worse, Sean makes it worse! It's like magic! I was trying really, really hard to think friendly, generous thoughts about Sean, but it was like being kicked in the teeth.

"Oh sure," Eric said. "I mean, you gotta do what you gotta do."

"Exactly," Sean said. I don't know if he missed the irony or just thought it couldn't be ironic when anyone agreed with him about something, but he leaned back in his chair again, looking satisfied. "Have you guys thought about my offer?"

His *offer*? It's not like he was thinking about buying us each a new car! So conceited. On the plus side, he wasn't making it harder to tell him no.

"Yeah," I said. Eric nodded.

"And?"

"And . . ."

This is our only chance, I thought, feeling weirdly calm. *Eric and I probably won't ever get another chance to do something like this.*

"Guys, seriously, why'd you come over?" Sean said, his voice sounding less annoyed, and also less annoying. "It's about DefenderCon, am I right?"

"Yeah, it is," I said.

"Awesome!" Sean grinned and quickly rubbed his hands together up and down.

He looked genuinely excited, which made him seem much nicer, and which also made me feel like a giant turd since we were about to shut him down.

Me and Eric. Me and Eric. Not me and Eric and Sean!

I resisted the urge to take a deep breath, which was hard, because now we were talking about the real thing and doing it my way by being honest, and there was no getting around the fact that Sean had actual human feelings that could get hurt.

Too late to back out now, though.

He leaned forward and put his hands on his knees. Ugh, he

was like a happy puppy! Why couldn't he not be a jerk and just be like this every time he talked to us? Every other time, anyway.

"It would be really cool for all three of us to go—" Eric said.

"I know!"

"But here's the thing."

Sean's face froze. It wasn't like his expression changed from excited to mad, it just stopped moving at all, in any way.

"We've been planning this for a long time—"

"—since right after Christmas," I said.

"Yeah. And the thing is, it's kind of a big deal for us, because I'm moving away at the end of the year." Eric was totally keeping it together. We had ice in our veins.

Me and Eric. Eric was moving away. Me and Eric. Not me and Eric and Sean. Not Sean.

"Meaning what?" Sean said, and this time his voice wasn't happy. It wasn't anything—he sounded like a robot. His face wasn't frozen anymore, but it was just as blank as his voice.

"Meaning this is, like, our last chance to do something we really want to do together before Eric . . . leaves."

"Uh-huh," Robot Sean said. He leaned back in his chair and crossed his arms.

"It's really important to us," Eric said, and I caught his eye and nodded.

"So . . . we're gonna go by ourselves this time," I said.

"This time." There was something in Sean's voice when he said that, like a little bit of an edge.

"Yeah, this time," I said.

"So that's it."

"Well, no," Eric said. "We could, you know, do some other comic book thing."

"Totally!" I said.

Sean looked at me, then at Eric, then back at me. For a second I seriously thought he might cry, but then he did the opposite and smirked. It was a hard, mean-looking smirk too.

"Yeah, that's not happening."

I guess I should have been ready for anything, but after seeing Sean act like a person I actually thought I could tolerate, or even like, it really stung to hear that mocking voice again so soon.

"Uh . . . okay," I said, suddenly off-balance. "We were just trying to—"

Sean cut me off with a hard slash of his hand.

"Whatever. I wasn't serious anyway."

"Um, yes you were," Eric said with a frown.

"Nope. I can't believe you fell for it. Suckers."

Okay, hurt feelings are one thing, but being a huge jerk about it is something else.

"Yeah, dude, you totally got us." Eric sounded as mad as I was starting to feel, but I decided to try one more time.

"Dude, seriously, the Rocket Cats show—"

"What *about* the Rocket Cats show?"

Sean said that in such a harsh, bullying tone that I leaned backward so I could get farther away from him, and my stomach instantly twisted itself into a knot.

"Nothing." I stood up, and a second later Eric was standing too. "We just thought maybe you'd understand it's nothing personal—"

"Oh yeah, right."

"*Stop interrupting me!*" I said. "It's not about you, you know!"

"Obviously." Sean waved an arm dramatically toward the door. "Since it's not about me, you might as well get out of here."

"Fine by me," I said, feeling angry and confused. What the heck was going on??

"Yeah, we're out," Eric said. Sean watched us as we walked across the room, but then he spoke just before we reached the door.

"It's gonna suck for you guys if Mr. D finds out about your crappy plan, though."

Okay, we'd seen the Secret Nice Version Sean, but that was over; this was Sean at His Most Evil. I couldn't help it—I totally froze up with panic at the thought of getting in that kind of trouble—but that was when Eric showed why people should always stick with their best friends.

"Why?" Eric said. I had no idea what he was getting at, but it gave me the time I needed to pull myself together. Sean clearly had no idea what Eric was getting at either.

"What do you mean, *why?* Do you *want* to get expelled?"

"No," Eric said. "Do you want everyone at school to know you like the Rocket Cats?"

Oh. *Oh.*

Sean stared at Eric for a solid five seconds without saying anything, and I had to fight the urge to squirm or look down at my feet. We were blackmailing Sean! I'd never done that to anyone before.

Me and Eric, me and Eric, me and Eric . . .

"It's not—" I said.

"It's not *what?*" Sean snapped at me, and that actually helped. It's easier to blackmail someone who's not being all friendly and happy.

"It's not a *bad* thing to like the Rocket Cats, you know." And suddenly I was being honest with Sean again! But in a weirdly dishonest way because we were fighting fire with fire! My head started to hurt. "It's not like we'd be publicly dragging you or something."

"We *like* the Rocket Cats," Eric said with a shrug. "And so do you."

Sean made an *nnnnggghhh* sound.

"I mean, you said it yourself," Eric said. "It'd be *so cool*."

Eric was really twisting the knife. Backward. Or counter-clockwise. Or something.

"And it *is* cool that you wear a Rocket Cats shirt to bed," I said.

I crossed my arms, partly to try to look tough, but mostly to hide the fact that my hands were shaking. Saying stuff that's true if you look at it one way, but threatening if you look at it another way was *so hard!*

"Okay, so you're gonna be like that, whatever," Sean said, his voice getting higher with each word. He flapped his hands at us like he was shooing a fly. "Get out of my house, losers."

"Not until you swear you won't say anything," I said. My

voice came really, really, really close to quivering, and I had to clench pretty much every muscle in my body to stop it.

"I don't care what you queers do!" Sean barked. "Go ahead and make out at the conference or whatever, just get out of here before I beat your faces in!"

Good enough. I was too angry and scared and rattled to keep talking anyway, and when I grabbed Eric and pushed him toward the door I saw his hands shaking too, so it was definitely time to go.

We left without another word.

SEAN'S MOM WAS NOWHERE IN SIGHT, so we broke with protocol and didn't thank her or anything before getting out of there. I went down the porch steps two at a time, and Eric didn't even bother, jumping all the way down all four steps at once. He landed on the front path in a crouch, putting down both hands to steady himself as I used my momentum to break into a run. We hit the sidewalk at full speed and didn't stop running until we'd run four full blocks, all the way to where Sean's street dead-ended into Zajac Road. Cars whizzed past us as we hunched over with our hands on our knees, sucking wind.

"What just happened??" Eric said between big, whooping gulps of air.

"I don't even know," I said, gasping.

"That was," Eric said, "terrifying!"

"I know, right?" I said. "What's gonna happen?"

"I'm supposed to know?" Eric straightened up slowly. "Wow, look at your hands!"

By then I was standing up straight too, and I realized I was running my hands through my hair without thinking about it, so I brought them down to eye level. They were shaking.

"Whoa," I said, and my voice felt shaky too. I felt sweat running down my temples.

Eric came over, wrapped an arm around my shoulders, and shook me back and forth.

"You didn't crack under the pressure!" he said.

"Well, almost."

"Not me."

"Oh please, you lie like a rug."

"Matt. Nobody says 'lie like a rug.'"

"I do. I'm somebody."

"Yeah, you are."

We hugged, and of course someone had to blare their car horn as they drove past, making us jump. We glared at the back of the car as it disappeared down the street.

"Jerks," Eric said.

"No kidding," I said as I looked at my watch. "Ugh, I should probably go home. I still have to finish my math homework."

"You want to grab a cookie at my house first?"

"Definitely." One of the benefits of Eric's mom being a pastry chef was that she was always testing new dessert recipes and letting me and Eric eat the results. One of the drawbacks was getting new jobs in cities on the other side of the country, of course.

"Is it a new recipe?"

"Yeah, it's chocolate and hazelnut and something else."

"Dude. I'll race you there!"

We ran the last two blocks to Eric's house, reenergized by the thought of cookies. His mom was out being a pastry chef or whatever, so we kept our Day of Evil Behavior alive by ignoring the house rules and bringing our cookies into the living room. A bookcase with a zillion cookbooks took up most of one wall, and I couldn't help wondering when Eric's mom would start packing them up for the move.

"What do you think?" Eric said through a mouthful of cookie.

I nodded, wiped my sweaty face on my shoulder, then swallowed hard. "Really good. And I don't even like hazelnuts."

Eric nodded and handed me another cookie.

"What do you think about what Gabi said?" I said after taking a small bite.

"About what?" Eric said.

"About, you know, thinking we're gay."

Eric chewed a bite of cookie and shrugged. "I don't know. She's definitely the nicest person who's told us we're gay."

"Yeah, and she didn't say it like it's a BAD thing, you know what I mean? Everybody else says YOU'RE GAY like it means you've just been infected by a zombie or something."

"Seriously."

"And you're right about Sean." I rubbed my forehead with the heel of one palm. "He does say it like that."

"Right. Can I ask you a question?" Eric said.

"Dude, that's never a good way to ask a question," I said. "Now I'm all worried about what you're gonna ask."

"Yeah, I know, and this conversation was so not awkward at all until now! Seriously, though."

"Sure, go ahead."

"Do you think you might be gay?"

"I don't think so," I said. "I mean, I don't have a girlfriend or anything, but I wouldn't MIND having a girlfriend."

"Me neither."

"Would it bother you if I was?"

"I don't think so. Would it bother you if I was?"

"No. Are you?"

Eric shook his head.

"I guess that's okay," I said. Eric laughed, which made me laugh too.

"Wait, why are we talking about how it's okay to not be gay?" he said.

"*I'm* not. And you're not either."

"Isn't blackmailing people kind of terrible?" I sank even deeper into the couch, which was extremely squishy and soft. It was a really good movie-watching couch.

"Not if the other person is blackmailing you first. Remember that part?"

"Yeah. Still." I breathed out a big, lip-flapping gust of air, *PBBBBBBBDBDBDBDBTTTHHHHH.*

"You should probably get going." Eric held up his left wrist in front of me and tapped on his watch with his other hand.

"Oh shoot, right." I dragged myself out from the smashed-down couch cushions and stood up. Eric got up and put his hands on my shoulders.

"It's gonna work," he said, shaking me forward and back for emphasis. "DefenderCon. It'll be *fine*."

"Okay."

I still felt like doom lay over the horizon, though.

"YOU LOOK GREAT, MATT, LET'S TAKE
a picture!"

"Dad. We already took pictures at home."

"Just one more in front of the school, please."

"DAD."

"It's the spring concert, Matt! March is a great time for pictures!"

I groaned.

"Honey," Mom said.

"Okay, okay, I'm sorry," Dad said as he stuck his phone in his pocket.

"Respect bodily autonomy, Dad."

"Yes, you're totally right, Matt."

To give credit where it's due, Mom and Dad really mean it

when they say they'll take no for an answer about stuff that's not really that important, like taking an endless number of pictures. That doesn't mean they won't be annoying about it first, though.

We were part of a stream of orchestra kids and families who were walking into the school, which always feels like a different place at night. For one thing, orchestra members go in through a smaller set of double doors off to the side of the building, while audience members have to walk past that entrance, go in through the big front doors, and turn into the auditorium. The fact that it's dark outside makes it feel brighter inside, even though the lights are all the same as when it's daytime.

Everyone's also dressed for orchestra, which isn't like marching band at all because we don't wear uniforms. We have to wear fancy clothes—white shirts with collars, black pants or skirts, and black dress shoes—but they're regular fancy clothes. So everyone in orchestra looks different too.

Just inside the doors a gang of girls surrounded Graysin Oh, who wasn't actually talking—he was just listening to everyone else talk. Maybe that was his secret. A couple of trumpet players were hanging out by the door leading to the auditorium stage, but Kenny wasn't one of them, and Sean was also nowhere to be seen, so I relaxed as I searched for Eric. The practice rooms were both occupied by woodwind players, and the only people in the band room were Skye Oh and a couple of the other flute players. I waved at them, but Skye was the only one who waved back. She just kept on talking with the other girls, though, so I decided to go back outside and wait for Eric.

I threaded my way through the other band geeks who were arriving and walked outside, stopping at the top of the steps leading up to the door. More people were milling around out there—families walking from the parking lot to the school, parents saying "good luck" and "break a leg" to kids as they went to their separate doors, and orchestra kids hanging out with their instrument cases in their hands. Everyone looked pretty happy, except for some of the non-orchestra kids who were obviously there because their parents were making them be there.

A car screeched to a stop at the end of the block, across the street from the school parking lot, and someone got out of the rear door, then walked over to the driver's window. Whoever it was started to lean down, like they were going to talk to the person driving, but as they were doing it the car pulled away, blew through the stop sign at the corner, turned right, and disappeared.

A bunch of families were getting out of their cars and walking toward the school, and a lot of them turned to look as the mystery person stood up and watched the car drive off. They all looked away when the person turned around and started walking slowly toward the school all alone, though. It looked like their family (or whoever was driving that car) wasn't staying for the concert, and I was feeling more and more awful about it until they walked into the light at the edge of the school parking lot and I realized it was Kenny.

Ugh. It was super weird to feel bad for Kenny, just like it'd been to hear Sean's mom talking trash about Sean; I still didn't like it. Luckily, I also recognized two of the other people walking in from the parking lot: Eric and his pastry chef mom. They both waved, and I waved back as I went down the steps and met them on the sidewalk.

"Hi, Matt." Eric's mom preferred being called "Ellie," which made sense since that was her name. She had a complicated smile on her face, kind of happy and sad at the same time, but it was a friendly complicated smile, so I smiled back even though I was still mad at her for deciding to move.

"Hi, Ellie."

"Hey," Eric said as he propped his arm on my shoulder and leaned against me, which might have tilted me off-balance if I hadn't already braced myself for it.

"Last orchestra thing of the year, huh?" I said.

"Yeah." Eric smiled, but it was a complicated smile just like his mom's, and I knew we were thinking the same thing.

Last orchestra thing of any year for the two of us.

Ellie reached out with both hands and touched us each on one shoulder.

"Well . . . have a great show, guys," she said. "You're going to be great."

"Thanks, Mom," Eric said as Ellie kissed him on one cheek. At the same time I saw Kenny walk past out of the corner of my eye. He was eyeballing Eric and his mom with an incredibly sad expression, and he caught me looking at him just before I could turn away. The memory of seeing him stare at Graysin flashed through my mind, and it occurred to me that repeatedly seeing things Kenny didn't want me to see was probably a bad idea.

Kenny's face turned red all at once, and he lurched up the steps and into the building.

"Welp, Kenny's here," I said.

"Oh, okay. Party's over, huh?"

"Maybe it's just gonna be a different kind of party."

"Yeah, if by 'different,' you mean 'terrible.'"

"Come on, let's go inside." I threw my arm all the way over

Eric's shoulder, and as we headed into the building I felt the most bizarre kind of fear. I was used to being afraid what Kenny might try to do to us, but after seeing this sad and unhappy side of Kenny and actually feeling sorry for him, I was afraid that once Eric was gone and I was alone, I'd be as miserable as Kenny looked.

We walked through the door, and of course Kenny the Miserable One was standing just inside it, ready to stick out his foot and trip me, which is exactly what he did. I stumbled forward, and I probably would have fallen on my face if Eric hadn't braced his feet and reached up to grab my hand that was resting on his shoulder. We spun partway around, and I had to put my free hand down on the floor for a second, but I stayed on my feet and managed not to crash into anyone. Kenny laughed.

"Is that gonna be your wedding dance, losers?" he said.

"No, it's our dance of sadness that you still exist," Eric snapped back.

One of the girls circling Graysin laughed—it was Nora Dairman—and when I looked over there I saw the whole circle of people was watching us. Kenny's face turned dark red—it was like a face-shaped blood clot—and he scowled.

"What are you laughing at, Nora?" he said.

"Oh, there are so many things," Nora said cheerfully. By now everyone in the hallway was listening, and I wondered where the heck Mr. D was, because the look on Kenny's face was starting to scare me.

"Yeah, well, you better shut up."

"Why don't you?" Nora said. "I mean, seriously, if anyone around here should get married, it's you and Sean."

The whole hallway burst into laughter, and Kenny shrank back against the wall with a wide-eyed, deer-in-the-headlights look on his face. It was seriously turning into the Year of Seeing Kenny Do Things I'd Never Seen Him Do Before.

"Great, I'm happy to hear you all in such a good mood!"

Mr. D was preceded by his voice, but I looked over my shoulder just in time to see him turn the corner from the band room, grinning like he was having the time of his life. He probably was, too—for some reason he really likes the spring concert, maybe because it involved less marching. The laughter in the hallway quieted down, but the Kenny-fueled tension was mostly gone.

"It's time to warm up, musicians, let's go!"

I looked back at Kenny as Mr. D. spun on his heel and led the lemming migration back into the band room. Sean appeared in the doorway and skidded to a halt just inside, right next to Kenny. He was breathing hard, like he'd been running, and he looked at Kenny with no idea what he'd just missed.

"Hey, man, sorry I'm—"

Kenny cut Sean off by giving him a shove, and I mean a hard one, right in the chest.

"WHOA!"

Sean pinwheeled his arms and staggered back all the way across the hallway and into the opposite wall. He grunted as his back hit the cement, and slapped his palms against the wall to keep from falling down.

"Dude, what is *that* for—"

"*Leave me alone*," Kenny said in a voice that was low, but still terrifying.

"Matt, let's go," Eric said into my ear, and that sounded good to me. This was probably another thing Kenny wouldn't want me to see, and I'd had my fill.

"Kenny, what's going on—*ow!*"

"*Don't touch me, you queer!*"

We turned to go and immediately bumped into a cluster of four or five people who'd also been watching Kenny turn on

Sean. They all kind of jumped, like we'd released them from a magic spell, then joined us in hustling toward the band room, where the sounds of tuning instruments were getting loud. I had a sick feeling in my stomach. I wasn't sure what had just happened, but whatever it was, it felt really, really bad.

WHEN THE SPRING CONCERT was over, we started marching band practice again. We do that every year, and it always feels like kind of a big deal because we know we'll be performing at graduation, but practicing for the World of Amazement festival was on a whole other level. It was *intense.* It didn't help that Kenny had kicked Sean out of their two-person clubhouse for real. Sean kept asking Kenny what was wrong until Kenny threatened to beat him up, right in front of the whole cafeteria. So yeah, marching band practice felt more like a pit of vipers than ever, and it didn't take long for the vipers to start biting.

There are rules about playing instruments, and the big one is don't mess with someone else's instrument, even if it's the easiest instrument on the face of the planet like bass drum. You just don't do it; it's like a respect thing. But Sean McKenna didn't have any respect for anyone, especially since his friend breakup with Kenny, so it's not like it was a giant shock when he decided to level up with the hostility at band practice, especially with Mr. D cracking the whip like he was.

I didn't think he'd do it by breaking one of the cardinal marching band rules, though. I mean, seriously. You don't mess with someone else's instrument, ever!

BA-BUMP.

When Sean reached over and hit my bass drum twice, I was so surprised that I missed the start of the next measure, at which point Sean hit my drum again, *BA-BUMP.* He was completely off, of course. That part wasn't surprising at all.

"Hey!" I said, my stomach suddenly churning. "What are you doing, Sean?"

"Play it right," Sean said in a strict-sounding tone, like he'd been magically turned into the band director.

"I am playing it right. Why are you playing it wrong, and on my drum?"

"Because you obviously can't get it right, loser."

"You're the one who never gets it right!"

"Dude, you're so gay, I—"

"So gay?? What does that even mean?"

"Maybe if you opened your eyes wider you could—"

"Open my eyes wider??"

It was raining, which was super unusual for spring, so we were rehearsing in the band room. That was probably good, because getting into a stupid argument while marching probably would have ended in a fifteen-band-geek pileup. Sean and I were both hopelessly lost on the song, though—finding out someone's a homophobic racist does that to me—and Mr. D was going to notice sooner or later.

"Whoa, stop, wait a minute." Drabek dropped his baton hand to his side and slashed the air a couple of times with his other hand.

Okay then, sooner, not later.

"What's going on, bass drummers?" Mr. D put his hands on his hips and glared at the back of the room.

"Nothing," Sean said with a totally fake-casual expression on his face.

"Uh-huh, sure," Mr. D said, not looking very convinced. "As long as nothing's going on, how about playing your own drum, Sean?"

Busted! And Sean knew it—he kept up the fake "everything's cool" expression, but I saw his Adam's apple go up and down. Dude was swallowing hard.

"It's not Sean's fault, Mr. Drabek," Eric said. "He can't help it that he's not that good."

"Cut it out," Drabek said, pointing a finger at Eric. Mr. D's voice didn't sound happy, and Eric shut up right away. That put the smirk back on Sean's face, but Drabek wiped it right back off.

"Get it together, Sean," he said, still using his "I'm not happy" voice. "The competition's getting closer every day."

"Come on, Mr. D, what about him?" Sean said, sticking his finger way too close to my ear, like a bony mosquito. I batted it away with my hand.

"See?" Sean said, throwing both hands in the air. "Matt's the one who's touching people, Mr. D!"

"Both of you knock it off, NOW," Mr. Drabek said, which was super unfair to me, but unlike Sean, I knew when to not push it. Sean opened his mouth to say something else, but closed it when Mr. D stared him down.

"You don't have the luxury of not needing to practice, Sean," Mr. D said. He was obviously mad, so nobody said anything out loud, but we all looked around at each other with big, open-mouth expressions on our faces, and someone made a very quiet, cackling, *oh-ho-ho-ho-ho-hooooooo* sound.

"Okay, gang, from the top," he said, raising his baton. Eric turned his head just far enough to make one-eyed eye contact with me, and we shook our heads just a tiny bit. I started to flip back through the ridiculously easy bass drum music, but Sean interrupted me by poking me in the shoulder with a drum mallet. I didn't want to risk the Wrath of Drabek again, so I looked at Sean out of the corner of my eye.

"That was so uncool," he said in a harsh whisper, also looking at me from the corner of his eye, and whispering out of the side of his mouth.

"Oh yeah, I was the one hitting your drum, huh?" I whispered back.

"You were playing it wrong."

"It's not my fault you're such a terrible drummer."

"Oh, you're dead, queer boy," he said. "You think you can blackmail me and get away with it, but you have no idea. You're so dead."

Welp. That sounded promising.

PRING WAS TURNING OUT TO BE
kind of a dumpster fire, so it was a relief when
Ms. Bruce came through with a cool new project
for physics class.

"Good morning, class! Any Skykiller questions today? I'll
take three. Matt!"

Sixth grade was the first time I'd ever gotten a new teacher
halfway through the school year, and at first I was sad because
I'd always liked Mr. Philips, but Ms. Bruce turned out to be one
of the best teachers ever. Mom and Dad said she must have just
graduated from teacher college (or whatever you call it) because
those are the only teachers who look for jobs that start right after
New Year's, and they said it like it was a bad thing, but I didn't
get it. She wasn't incredibly stuck-up like Ms. Oates, she didn't

completely ignore everything anyone said like Mr. Castillo, and she was the only teacher I've ever had who knows as much about the Skykiller movies as I do. She even lets us try to stump her in class, if we want.

"What's the name of Spark Dahlen's astromech droid?" I said, hand still in the air.

"Minispark! Reggie!"

Reggie Halko sat next to Skye Oh, who was staring at the front of the room with her eyes half-closed and her head pulled into her neck like a turtle. Skye was not a Skykiller fan. Reggie, on the other hand, was a superfan.

"In *Rise of the Insurgency*, who's the leader of the rebels stationed on Declan Five?"

Ooh, good one, Reggie.

"Captain Atteberry! Aaaaaand—" Ms. Bruce waved her finger in a circle, then brought it down super fast. "Eric!"

"What was the name of the city where the bounty hunters caught up with Barkley Baptiste in *Fallen Rebel*?"

Awesome question, as expected.

"Ha, that's a hard one! Let's see . . . right, it was Ferrante! And Barkley got away!"

Someone coughed, and the cough sounded suspiciously like

it was actually the word "dorks," but it bothered me less in Ms. Bruce's class than it usually did.

"Okay, people, we're going to start a new project today, and trust me, it's a fun one."

An excited murmur filled the room. The best thing about Ms. Bruce's class was how she taught stuff like the laws of physics. She took these "gremlins," which were actually super-weird stuffed animals she made herself, and put them onto things like a bike wheel on a stand or a car on a track. Then she'd demonstrate things like centripetal force or momentum by spinning the wheel or crashing the car, sending the gremlin flying through the air. Hopefully "fun" meant "lots of gremlins."

"It's a group project—"

The whole class said some version of "noooooooooooo" at the same time.

"—Oh, come on, it's not like this is the first group project we've done this year. Anyway, we're going to make catapults!"

The group "noooooooooo" turned into more of an excited babble. Catapults are for throwing stuff! *Please say we'll get to throw gremlins!*

Ms. Bruce passed around a handout with all the details as she explained. Working in teams of four people, we had to make catapults using Popsicle sticks (!?) from the design specs on the handout.

"The kind of catapult we'll be making is called a mangonel. You can make yours as small or as big as you want to, but keep in mind that you're using sticks to make it, so the longer the beam is, the more you'll have to worry about its structural integrity!"

Eric turned around and silently mouthed the words "awesome project," and I did a low-key double thumbs-up without lifting my hands off my desk.

"I'm looking forward to seeing what direction you all take with your projects, and here's some extra incentive: We're going to have a contest to see whose catapult throws a standard projectile the farthest!"

Ms. Bruce walked quickly back to her desk, opened a drawer, pulled out a brand-new gremlin, and raised it over her head with one hand while making little waving motions around it with her other hand.

The room broke out in clapping and cheers, and Ms. Bruce had to clap her hands a couple of times to get everyone to shut up.

"Okay then, let's take a few minutes to form up into groups, and let me know if you need my help!"

I gave Eric a fist bump, since obviously we'd be on the same team. Filling out the rest of the team could be a problem—not being even a little bit popular caused a lot of problems like that— but this time, for a change, it wasn't.

"Duuuuuudes!" Hector said, high-fiving me, Eric, and the air as he and Jack came over and slid their stuff onto our table. "Roomies working on a group project, this is gonna be epic!"

"Okay, Hector, calm down," Jack said in his droopy-dog way. I cracked up.

"No one's more calm than you, Jack," Eric said, giving Jack a handclasp on the shoulder.

"Good job organizing your groups, people!" Ms. Bruce said. "And now, a demonstration!"

She pulled out a box from the spot under her desk where her legs would go if she ever sat down, which she hardly ever did, and in just a couple of minutes she'd assembled a real catapult right there on the lab table at the front of the room. It was made of wood and was a couple of feet tall, with a flat base, two trian- gular sides, wooden rods connecting the sides at both the top points and bottom middles of the triangles, and a long vertical arm attached to the center of the base. The end of the arm had a wooden spoon attached to it.

"As you can see, I took a shortcut by building this catapult out of pine," Ms. Bruce said. "So you shouldn't necessarily rely on it as a model for yours, because you're going to have some different structural concerns to think about. But you *will* test your catapults by doing the exact same thing I'm about to do right now, which is . . ."

She took the gremlin, which was basically just a furry lump the size of a lime with googly eyes, floppy hands and feet, and a pipe cleaner antenna on it, and put it into the bowl of the spoon. Then she held down the base of the catapult and pulled the top end of the wooden spoon lever back until it was almost flat on the tabletop.

Ms. Bruce looked at us with a big smile.

"Ready?"

"YES!" we all said at once.

She let go of the lever, which snapped back up like a clock hand going super fast. When it hit the crosspiece it stopped short, and the gremlin flew out of the wooden spoon like a furry little cannonball. It hit the wall with a *thwump*, then hit the floor with another *thwump*. I was really impressed that none of the gremlin's body parts fell off.

There was more cheering and clapping as Ms. Bruce picked up the gremlin and walked back to her desk.

"One more thing," she said, reaching into her catapult box with both hands. "You'll need to test your catapult designs with a projectile that's regulation size and weight, of course, so you can use these."

She took out a pile of beanbags. They were the kind you get in a little mesh bag when you buy one of those "learn how to juggle" kits, and they were almost the exact same size as the catapult gremlin.

"Do not lose these!" Ms. Bruce warned as she put a beanbag on each group's table. "I don't have extras, so if you lose yours, you'll have to replace them yourselves."

We spent the rest of the class collecting supplies from the bins of stuff Ms. Bruce put out on the big lab table. There were actual Popsicle sticks, but there were also big tongue depressors, and we grabbed a bunch of each. Everybody already had their own rolls of tape and bottles of glue, but we also got some zip ties and rubber bands.

"Did you guys hear about Kenny?" Jack said in a low voice, looking from side to side like he was in a spy movie.

"You mean about him threatening to rip Sean's head off?" I said as Eric, Hector, and I all leaned forward to listen.

"No, but it kind of relates to that—Emma told me that a friend of hers from theater camp knows someone who saw Kenny in the park by the lake, and he was kissing . . . *another guy.*"

"Whoa," I said.

"Whoa is right," Hector said. "How did Kenny find someone willing to actually kiss him?"

"Is your friend's friend's friend's friend sure it was a *human* boy?" Eric said.

Hector and Jack both cracked up, but Eric and I exchanged a confused look. I was having a short-but-intense argument with myself about whether I should mention seeing Kenny stare at Graysin that one time, but I decided against it, partly to spare Graysin from any rumors, but mostly because telling people about that seemed like a decent way to get Kenny to tear my head off.

Kenny going off on Sean right after Nora suggested they were gay was already common knowledge, but that wasn't my fault.

"But is Kenny, you know, gay?" Jack said.

"Jack, be serious." I crossed my arms. "Your friend's friend's friend's friend said they saw this? How do we know *that* person's real?"

THE **BOYS** IN THE **BACK ROW**

"I don't know, but you know what happened before the spring concert," Jack said. "Is it just a coincidence?"

"Gay or straight, it'd be good news either way," Eric said. "Maybe having a boyfriend would make him less evil."

"You know, that's what happened with my cousin who used to be all mean to me and stuff," Hector said. "He started seeing this girl, and they were, like, super into each other, and he stopped messing with me every time we went to his house!"

"That *would* be nice," Jack said.

"My cuz isn't all bad, though—he's the one who got me into Galactic Herald."

"Galactic Herald is awesome!" I said. "I just got their new album."

"Aw man, I haven't even heard any of—"

Eric elbowed Hector in the side as Ms. Bruce walked over to our table.

"How's it going, guys? Have you assigned roles for your team yet?"

All four of us hunched our heads down into our necks, which is basically like saying "GUILTY, WE'RE GUILTY," but I still managed to say "er, not yet, we've been focusing on materials."

"Well, I'm not worried about you four, but make sure you discuss who's doing what before the end of class, okay?"

"Okay!" we said in unison, which was weird, but . . . nice?

It was like we weren't just field trip roommates, but also a real team.

I WASN'T ALL THAT USED TO PEOPLE RAN-domly coming over to my house, so whoever it was that rang the doorbell would have been a surprise as long as it wasn't Eric. I had a sudden paranoid moment when I thought it might be *Sean*, ready to light our house on fire or something, but it wasn't Eric or Sean, it was Hector. Hooray, a nonthreatening surprise. A pleasant surprise, even, which was also a surprise. It was like a wormhole of surprise.

"Dude, let's hear it!" Hector, as usual, had the biggest, toothiest grin on his face and was bouncing slightly on his toes. He also had a rake and a box of trash bags in his hands, which was less usual.

"Uh . . . hi?"

"Hey! Can I come in?"

"Sure. What's with the rake?" I said as I stepped aside and waved him in.

"Yard work," he said, rubbing the fingertips on one hand together. "Money."

"Oh. Right. I knew that."

"Yeah, I've seen you mowing lawns and stuff," Hector said cheerfully.

"I don't bring my own lawn mower, though."

"Well, yeah, who drags their own lawn mower around?"

Hector scuffed his feet twice on the doormat, leaned his rake against the porch railing, put the trash bags on the porch next to the rake, then stuck his hand in my direction, elbow bent at a right angle. I stuck my hand out too, and he shook it firmly, nodded, and finally came into the house. His hand was all sweaty, but whatever, you gotta respect the whole moneymaking thing, especially since I needed to do some moneymaking of my own if I was going to buy any souvenirs at DefenderCon.

"When are we gonna listen to it?" he said, looking eagerly at me.

"Listen to what? It'd probably help if, you know, I knew what you're talking about."

"The new Galactic Herald album! You have it, right?"

"Oh, that. Yeah, I do."

"Is it on your phone? Do you have a Bluetooth speaker? I brought mine, just in case." Hector pulled a barrel-shaped speaker with a blue rubber cover out of his jacket pocket.

"Er, well, no, we don't need a speaker."

"No worries, I'm cool with listening on your computer!"

"Okay. We, er, have to go downstairs . . ."

"—out-and-out lies, it's maddening. And the moderators, holy—"

Hector tilted his head in the direction of the kitchen, where Mom and Dad were talking about everything terrible about the world—racism, sexism, the usual stuff. "Toxic masculinity" was the major topic lately.

"Dude, you're eavesdropping. On my *parents*."

"What, you don't listen in on your parents? I do it all the time," Hector said, sounding like that was just totally normal. "Wow, your mom and dad are intense!"

"Tell me about it."

"Are they talking about the presidential debate?"

"Yeah. You have to admit, that debate was completely bananas."

"Yeah, my dad just yelled '¡no sabes nada!' at the TV over and over again."

"Yup, it was bad." I turned my head toward the kitchen. "HEY, MOM. HEY, DAD!"

"Easy with the yelling, babe," Mom said. Hector cracked up.

"What?" I said, irritated and embarrassed.

"Babe!" Hector said, laughing and holding his stomach with both hands. "Dude, that's so *cute!*"

"All right, all right, cut it out," I said. "Hang on a minute."

I walked through the living room and stuck my head into the kitchen, where Mom was holding a magazine article out for Dad to look at. They were both laughing.

"Isn't that just perfect?" Mom said.

"Spot-on. This might be my favorite political cartoon ever."

"Hey, Mom. Hey, Dad," I said.

"Thank you for not bellowing at us from across the house," Dad said. "Who was that at the door?"

"A friend. Can he stay over for a while?"

"Honey, you know Eric's always welcome here," Mom said. "Wait a minute, when you say 'a friend,' do you mean . . ."

"It's not Eric."

Mom and Dad turned in their chairs and looked at me in unison, which was always funny, even though it was also a tiny bit creepy.

"Not Eric?" Dad said in the kind of voice you might use to say *"unicorns are real?"*

"Honey! A new friend, that's so great!" Mom tossed the magazine onto the table and raised her arms in a V shape, which of course is exactly when Hector decided to poke his head into the kitchen too, because I obviously wasn't embarrassed enough already.

"Hi," he said, standing close enough to me that our shoulders were touching.

"Hello! Welcome!" Dad bounced up out of his chair so fast that it looked like he was doing a jumping jack, took two fast steps toward us, and stuck out his hand. I halfway expected Hector to back away in terror, but he gave Dad a patented Hector Morales grin instead.

"Thanks," Hector said. "I'm Hector."

"Steven Park," Dad said. "Matt's dad."

"Hi, Hector!" Mom was just as terrifyingly perky as Dad. She reached out, grabbed both of Hector's hands in her hands, and pumped all four hands up and down seven or eight times. "I'm Jen. It's so good to meet you!"

"Hi, Mrs. Park," Hector said, bobbing his head up and down a couple of times. Mom and Dad paused their campaign of embarrassment to smile goofily at each other, and Hector took the chance to grin at me and throw an elbow into my ribs.

"Ow," I said under my breath. "We're going downstairs," I said, louder.

"Do you guys want a snack or something?" Dad said, twisting his upper half and looking around the kitchen over his shoulder. "We might have some—"

"NO! I mean, no thanks, it's okay, no," I said, imagining Dad finishing off my social humiliation by pulling out a bag of sriracha-flavored kale chips or something. That would have been totally fine back in Cedarville, but Hector wasn't from Cedarville.

"How about you, Hector?" Dad said. He zeroed in on the cupboard next to the microwave.

"Sure," Hector said. "I mean, yes, thank you."

I *almost* warned Hector not to accept anything made with coconut flour, but I stopped myself because I didn't want to hurt Dad's feelings, then wondered exactly how I became the world's biggest goody-two-shoes doofus. Complicated moment.

"Here you go!" Dad handed Hector a box of green tea cookies. Okay, those were actually good.

"Thank you!" Hector flashed his big, toothy smile again, held the box up with both hands, and bobbed his head a couple of times.

"Dude, what are these?" Hector said under his breath as we went down the stairs.

"Green tea cookies. Try one."

"Never had 'em before," Hector said. Not ever having them before didn't stop him from having the box open by the time we got to the bottom of the stairs, though.

"You're lucky, these are good." I grabbed two cookies as Hector pulled the crinkly plastic tray partway out of the box. "Dad has some other stuff that's . . . uh, less good. What do you think?"

That last part came out more like "whuduhdoo thinmgh" because my mouth had a cookie stuffed in it. Hector didn't even try to talk through his full mouth, but he looked at me with his eyes very wide open and gave me a thumbs-up.

"Unggmmfh," he said, swallowing hard. "I mean, they're awesome!"

"I know, right?"

"Are these Korean? You're Korean, right?"

"No. I mean, yes. I mean, no, *they're* not Korean, but yeah, *I'm* Korean American. Dad says those"—I pointed a thumb at the cookies as we got to the bottom of the stairs—"are American rip-offs of a Japanese thing."

"Huh," Hector said, walking around the room and looking at stuff. "Like burritos."

"What about burritos?" I sat in front of my computer, woke it up from sleep mode, and opened the music app.

"Burritos are a made-up American thing." Hector stopped in front of the drawing of Petra Ursu taped to the wall over my futon and pointed at it. "This is really good!"

"Thanks. So . . ."

I was interrupted by the guitar riff at the start of "The Watcher," the first song on the new album by—

"Galactic Herald!" Hector held a cookie up in the air, exactly like the silvery alien on the cover of their first album, *Worlds within Worlds*, before cramming it dramatically into his mouth, and I couldn't help laughing. Hector laughed too, spraying a few crumbs in the air, then started air-drumming along. I already had the printed-out lyrics on my desk, so I picked them up, turned up the volume and started singing along. Hector joined in, which is when I found out he has a really good voice, and it was fun, even without Eric there, and for a second I wondered if maybe not everything would be terrible after he moved.

"DID YOU PACK A HAT? IT GETS
really sunny there," Dad said, looking up at the
sky as if the sun was about to explode right then.

"Yes."

"You've got your meds, right?"

"Dad. Yes. Please calm down."

Dad blew out a gust of breath. "It's times like these when I almost wish you had a phone."

"There's a way to make that wish come true, you—"

"We'll talk about it when you get home, Matt. Seriously."

Woo-hoo! Awesome! I mean, it would have been awesome if Eric and I didn't have a plan that would end up with us getting suspended at the very least. I was suddenly queasy, and felt a horrible urge to confess everything to Dad before we'd even done it.

"Thanks, Dad."

"There's Eric!" Dad waved as a car pulled up to the curb about halfway down the block from us. Eric and his mom both waved as they stopped. There were too many other cars already in front of school for Eric's mom to get past easily, so after Eric got out of the car with his stuff she did a three-point turn, which actually created a new roadblock behind her. Someone honked at her, and she honked back, and I wondered if a full-blown car horn war was about to break out, but she managed to turn around and head back the way she'd come without any more hostilities. Eric lurched toward us with a giant duffel bag slung across his back.

"Hey!" he said as he dumped the bag on the sidewalk next to my suitcase and backpack. "Hi, Mr. Park!"

"Hey, Eric!" Dad said. "Okay, guys, can you handle it on your own from here?"

"Absolutely," Eric said.

"Yup," I said, partly because Eric and I had stuff to discuss, and partly because I felt a totally bananas urge to say "next time I see you I'll probably be suspended and kicked out of marching band!"

"Okay." Dad took a deep breath, and I could tell he was forcing himself to not hug me or kiss me on top of the head. Mom and Dad are both pretty good about that kind of thing, but I hugged him anyway, in a "we who are about to go on a super-long bus ride salute you" way.

"Are you nervous?" I asked Eric as Dad walked up the street and around the corner to the car.

"No, but you are," Eric said as he unzipped his duffel bag, pulled out a backpack, and rezipped the duffel bag, which looked only a little less full than it did before.

"Dude, what are you talking about?"

"I'm talking about how you ask me if I'm nervous whenever *you're* nervous." Eric put on the backpack and grinned.

"Oh, come on, I don't do that."

"Every time."

"No."

"Are you nervous right now?"

. . .

"Well, yeah," I said after a minute.

"So am I!" Eric grabbed my hand, held it up in front of him, and high-fived it with his other hand.

"So awkward," I said, but I couldn't help laughing, nervous or not.

"ATTENTION, MUSICIAN-SCHOLARS!"

Principal Mendez was out on the sidewalk with her bullhorn. She has a thing about calling the marching band "musician-scholars," which most kids at school think is ridiculous, but I secretly like. Some of us actually do try to learn stuff, after all.

"Foghorn Mendez is about to blow," someone in the crowd said.

"YOU MAKE US PROUD, MUSICIAN-SCHOLARS!" she went on. "SHOW THE WORLD WHY HILLTOP SUMMIT HAS THE BEST MARCHING BAND IN THE STATE!"

Here's the thing about marching band: We have bullies, terrible students, and kids who'll totally lie to their parents and go to a comic book convention when they're supposed to be at World of Amazement instead, but most of us love being in the band. We're *proud* of being in the band, even though we're also super embarrassed about being in the band, which is why most of the band clapped and cheered really loudly when Mendez said what she said. All the parents that were there clapped and cheered too—all that band geek pride came from somewhere, after all.

Principal Mendez handed the bullhorn to Mr. D, waved with both hands, then turned and walked back into the building as Mr. D stepped into her place on the sidewalk.

"OKAY, LISTEN UP!" Mr. D bellowed. "BRING YOUR LUGGAGE TO MR. STELLA. HE'LL LOAD IT ONTO

THE BUS FOR YOU! WHEN YOU HEAR YOUR NAME, YOU CAN BOARD THE BUS!"

And so it began. Getting on the bus was slightly less nightmarish than expected because we had to wait until our names were called, so Eric and I ended up in pretty good seats—closer to the front of the bus than the back, but not *too* close to the front. We got lucky when the bully cohort (with Kenny, but minus Sean) headed for the back of the bus without paying any attention to us, but Sean gave us the serious evil eye as he passed our seats a couple of minutes later.

"Eh, don't worry about him," Eric said.

"Do I look worried?"

"Yes."

"No I don't."

"Okay, maybe it's, you know"—Eric made a circling motion in front of his face—"just how your face looks, then."

"Har dee har har."

The bus was super loud for a while—Mr. D had to tell us to stop yelling more than once—but the excitement of getting on the road wore off after half an hour, and everyone started getting crabby after a full hour, even with a bathroom break at a rest area thrown in. After two hours we stopped for lunch at EZ

Take-Out, where the burgers were awesome and the bathrooms were like a scene from a zombie apocalypse movie, and twenty minutes after getting back on the bus people started falling asleep, which meant I had some peace and quiet for the first time all day.

I'd brought three books on the trip, and I was halfway through my third time reading *Two Naomis*, an awesome book about two girls named Naomi whose lives get totally messed up when their totally selfish divorced parents (one mom and one dad) decide to start dating each other and eventually get married. So the girls start out not liking each other, but then become friends, and then sisters. It'd become my favorite book even though it had zero in the way of science fiction or fantasy— it made me think about how amazing it would be if Eric and I were brothers, even though I'd never tell anyone that—but I knew I couldn't just read it while everyone else was there to see because the cover was a picture of the two Naomis, and the Naomis are girls, and the only thing that's as bad for your social life as being the only boy piccolo player in the history of your school is . . . okay, nothing's as bad for your social life as that, but being a boy who reads books with girls on the cover (wearing stuff like flowery purple dresses, even) isn't a lot better.

Now, though? With people napping, reading their own books, or staring at their phones like zombies? Perfect timing. I opened the book to my favorite chapter—the one where the Naomis go to their favorite bakery for the last time—and I looked over at Eric, asleep in the seat next to me with his face mashed into a folded-up sweatshirt, which was mashed up against the bus window, and tried not to think about how horrible it was going to be when he moved. Then I started reading, but the bus felt sweaty and warm, and even though I can't fall asleep in cars I must have fallen asleep anyway, without meaning to. One second I was reading my book and the next second I was jerking awake at the sound of a voice right in my ear.

"Wake up, queer boy."

I opened my eyes, blinked in the hazy afternoon light coming through the bus windows, turned my head, and stared right into the face of Kenny Delacroix's gargoyle face, which was maybe two millimeters away from mine. I leaned away, grossed out, but I froze in horror when I saw what Kenny held in one of his gorilla paws. It was a book with a cover showing two girls in flowery dresses sitting on the porch of an apartment building.

My book.

Two Naomis.

GIVE THAT BACK!" I GRABBED wildly for the book, but Kenny pulled it just out of reach, cackling like a loon. He hooked one meaty arm over the top of the seat across the aisle from me, semi-crushing Hector's head before Hector could move out of the way, and started reading the back cover.

"Get off me, man!" Hector said, rubbing his head.

"'A moving tale of friendship, empathy, and girl power. I love the Naomis so much'—HOLY CRAP, THIS IS SO GAY! Are you actually a girl, Wang?"

Laughter broke out—too much laughter. It wasn't the whole band or anything like that, but it was enough of the band to make me feel super disappointed.

"Drop it, you jerk." Eric actually climbed over me to grab at the book, and he got his fingertips on it before Kenny yanked it away again.

"Sit down, Tiny Tim," he said.

"Oh geez, that's an amazing burn, I'm so mad," Eric said in a bored voice.

I jabbed Kenny in the armpit with my fingertips—desperation makes people do dangerous things, I guess—and Kenny grunted and dropped the book. I grabbed it off the floor and yelped as Kenny tried to stomp on my hand, missing by a few inches. I looked up at him in fear—I'll admit it, I'm not proud—just in time for him to grab the front of my shirt with his right hand, twist it up in a fist, brace his left hand against the back of my seat, and yank me up into a standing position, halfway strangling me in the process. His fist looked approximately the size of a bowling ball.

"You don't EVER touch me, Chicken Chow Mein—OW!"

Kenny let go of my shirt—oxygen!—and grabbed the back of his head. He twisted around and looked behind him at Skye Oh, who had an orange belt in aikido, and had apparently just smacked Kenny in the back of the head.

"Hey, that hurt!" Kenny said in a super-babyish voice. I would have laughed if I wasn't already so terrified and enraged. "You could have at least taken off your rings, Skye HO!"

Skye made a brushing motion on one shoulder and raised her hands about waist high.

"What did you call me?" she said in a deadly quiet voice.

"I called you Skye Ho, you slanty-eyed—OW!"

Kenny tried to block Skye, but holy cow, she was fast! WACK, she smacked Kenny on the side of the head (the one facing away from the teachers), then POOF, she vanished from my line of sight a nanosecond before Mr. D got up from *his* seat to stare back at us. Luckily everyone else was up and staring over the back of their seats too, so he couldn't see much.

"There better not be any nonsense going on back there," he said in his ominous tone of voice, bobbing and weaving to try to get a better view.

"Mr. D, Skye just karate kicked me," Kenny yelled like the yelling liar he was.

"I saw it," Sean said from somewhere behind me, almost making my head explode.

"Sean, you're such a liar!" I said.

"Sean, you're such a liar," he said in a nasal, super-high voice. "Why don't—OWWW, what—"

I couldn't see what happened, but I heard Skye's voice at low volume. Kenny was still looming over me like a killer grizzly bear, but he was also completely blocking me from Mr. D's view, so I risked ducking my head into the aisle and looking toward the back of the bus.

Skye was on the opposite side of the bus, one row back from ours, which explained how she could smack Kenny and get back in her seat so fast. Sean was hunched over next to her in the aisle, and at first I thought he was hiding behind Kenny like I was, but then I realized Skye had his wrist in some kind of complicated, painful-looking twist. She let go and he straightened up fast, not even trying to pretend his wrist didn't hurt.

"There's more where that came from, creepo."

What did she do to him? And would she be willing to teach me how to do it?

"KENNY. SEAN." Mr. D was *finally* walking back toward us. After it was all over, of course. "TAKE A SEAT."

I whipped my head around and ducked back into my seat just in time to avoid Kenny as he stomped toward the back of the bus. He kept that one clenched fist right in my face until he was past our row, but he couldn't punch me with Mr. D in motion. I looked at Eric and let my tongue hang out of my mouth like an overheated poodle.

Sean finally went back to his seat, wherever that was, but not without hearing some trash talk. A scramble of voices came from behind us.

"—your problem, dude—"

"—can't take a *girl*, you—"

"—knows karate or something—"

"—out of here, you're embarrassing—"

"—come *on*, I didn't say—ow . . ."

It wasn't a loud "ow"—I just barely heard it—but it was that high-pitched kind of "ow" that sounds like the person's really hurt and wasn't expecting it at all. The kind of "ow" *I've* said a few times at school until I trained myself not to. It hurt just to *hear* it.

"HEY!" Mr. D said in an "I am not messing around" shout, and the back of the bus went deathly silent. "KNOCK IT OFF!"

Ooh, that wasn't good. Mr. D isn't one of those prison warden teachers who gets super harsh whenever he possibly can, but when he gets shouting-level mad, look out. He's actually made people sit out performances before, and having to do that during this trip would be even more humiliating than usual.

"Whatever," Sean said in a low voice, but his voice shook a little, and then he actually walked toward the *front* of the bus and sat three rows ahead of us, next to Jeff Fisher, who was wearing headphones and didn't even turn to look when Sean sat down. Mr. D finally went back to his seat too.

That didn't mean anything was over, though. Probably the opposite. I looked down at my copy of *Two Naomis*, mad at myself for falling asleep while reading it, mad at myself for bringing it on the trip at all, and then, suddenly, super mad that I felt mad at *myself*, because why shouldn't I just get to read whatever books I want? People are horrible, especially Kenny and Sean.

"That went well," Eric said.

"Oh sure." I snorted. "Couldn't have gone better."

"I think Sean just set a record for being punched by people from the widest range of social groups at one time."

"Not feeling real sympathetic over here."

"Me neither. I mean, look at him."

Eric thrust his chin in Sean's direction. He was looking back at us. Only the top two-thirds of his head were visible—I couldn't see his mouth or chin—but his eyes were giving me a galaxy-class look of death.

"So this is what I'm worried about now," I said.

"Being murdered by Sean?"

"Not literally, but he still knows about our plan, right?"

"Right, but we still have leverage on him."

"Well, yeah, but . . ."

Eric didn't need to say it, because I was already thinking it. We *did* have leverage on Sean, because he'd definitely be super embarrassed about the Rocket Cats thing. Would that be enough to stop him anymore? And if it wasn't, when would Sean decide to sabotage Expedition DefenderCon? Would he do it during the bus ride, where we'd be trapped like goldfish in a bowl?

"He'll tell right before we leave," I said, not sure which I was feeling more, panic or gloom. "That'd be the most sadistic way to do it."

"Maaaaybe." Eric had that frowny expression on his face, the one that meant he was analyzing the situation instead of panicking.

"Not sure how. Also, stop using your 'don't panic' voice, it's annoying."

"I will if you stop panicking."

"I'm not panicking, I'm gently flipping out."

"Stop doing that, then. We still have Sean right where we want him."

"You think so?"

"Yeah. Watch."

Eric looked at Sean, raised his right hand with his index

finger pointing up and his thumb sticking straight out to the side, and stuck it on his forehead. Sean's eyes opened so wide you could see the whites all the way around the pupils. His hand didn't grab the back of his seat so much as instantly materialize there with the knuckles all white and everything. He rose maybe six inches out of his seat but then froze, darted his eyes toward the front of the bus, and slowly dropped back into his seat.

"Wow," I said as Eric dropped his hand. "I've never seen you do that before."

"That's just because I've never done it before," Eric said.

"Well, doy, that's because it's pure evil." I sighed. "We have become what we behold."

"I don't even know what that means, but my point is Sean's on Mr. D probation now. Would you want to come all this way and then have to sit and watch the competition with the teachers?"

"No way." I shuddered. "That would be the worst."

"At this point it'd be even worse for Sean."

"No doubt. It's just . . . I don't know. I don't want to be evil just because he's evil."

"Matt. We actually blackmailed him by *calling ourselves giant losers*."

"Yeah, but that doesn't mean it's cool for us to blackmail him with the Rocket Cats thing. We *like* the Rocket Cats."

"Uh, Matt, I hate to tell you, but that was your idea."

"Dude, no, that was your idea."

"Oh, right." Eric sighed. "Ugh, I hate it when you're right."

"Wow, so you hate life all the time, huh?"

"No, just once every couple of years."

I fanned the neck of my shirt to cool down—the sunlight pouring into the bus and the epic horribleness of how I woke up were both making me sweat like a pig. The bus rolled on, and there were a lot of wrapper-crumpling and chomping noises as everyone broke out energy bars, fruit, and other stuff to eat.

"You know what?" I said.

"I do know what," Eric said. "I know a bunch of different whats, actually."

"Just because Sean isn't coming over here to murder us right now doesn't mean he won't tell the teachers about our plan," I said. "It's not like he'd get in trouble for that."

"Sure he could. At this point Mr. D might even assume Sean's just lying."

"He wouldn't be, though."

"I don't think it even matters." Eric sat up and turned his

whole upper body to face me—as much as he could while sitting down, anyway. "Look at it this way: We're not troublemakers, right?"

"I guess."

"Especially you! I mean, seriously, everyone knows what a 'follow the rules' kind of person you are."

"Gee, thanks. Nice to know everyone thinks I'm a total suck-up."

"That's not my point. My point is, the teachers know. One time I even heard Mr. D and Mrs. Zeller talking about how you're the only kid in band they can trust to never lie to them."

"Really?"

Eric laughed, but in a good, Eric-like way. "See, I knew you'd like that. Yeah, really. Which means they always trust you, and—"

"—and right now they don't trust Sean."

"Right."

"Hopefully."

"Definitely!"

"Maybe."

Eric snorted. "Yeah. Maybe."

"But maybe not," I said. "I mean, look at him."

Sean was staring back at us *again*. How did he not have a giant cramp in his neck?

"I guess we have to wait and see what he does," I said.

"Yup."

I hate waiting. I hate it so, so much.

THE SUN, WHICH WAS GOING DOWN behind us, filled the Marching Band Horror Bus with gold-colored light, visible dust motes, and deep shadows. It felt like we'd been driving forever, and when we passed a huge sign that said "Next 3 Exits: World of Amazement" the bus erupted in cheering and whooping.

"*Three* exits," I said. "That's bananas. Do you remember there being three exits?"

"No, but I wasn't counting."

The first sign said "Next Exit: World of Amazement. Economy Parking, Car Rentals & Hotel Shuttle Transfers." A half mile later came the second sign, "Budget Parking & Off-Site Hotels."

"Are we at the airport?" Jack Browning said from somewhere

at the front of the bus. He sounded confused, but Jack sounds confused a lot. A barrage of mocking hoots came from the back of the bus, but Mr. D said "HEY" once, stopping it cold.

The third sign said "Next Exit: World of Amazement. Hotel of Amazement, On-Site Parking, Tour and Group Arrivals."

"That's us," Mr. D said, and the bus burst into cheers again.

The cheering stopped when we got off the freeway and drove straight into the worst traffic jam in the history of the world, or at least the worst one of my life. There were cars with license plates from a bunch of different states, taxis, buses like ours, much bigger buses with two levels, airport shuttles, and even more cars, all of them (including us) moving so slowly that pedestrians on the sidewalks were actually passing us.

The sidewalks were just as crowded as the roads, so it was like seeing a really slow-moving river of people flowing by an even more slowly moving river of cars right next to it. Everyone in the crowd seemed to have a World of Amazement hat, shirt, backpack, or shopping bag, and some people had all four, plus other stuff too. There were families of all shapes and sizes, roving packs of high school and college students, and huge mobs of kids like us being herded along by adults. Some of those adults looked like they were having fun, and some looked like they were stressed-out beyond belief. It was exciting and overwhelming at the same time.

Then we started seeing the DefenderCon people.

"Look!" I grabbed Eric's shoulder and pointed at the car that was slowly passing our side of the bus. It was a convertible with the top down, and there were two girls and two guys in it. They were obviously high schoolers—the guy in the back seat closest to us had a lot of acne, and the girl next to him was wearing a hat that said "Yu Ming High"—but what really caught our attention was the shirt on the other girl, who was in the front seat on the passenger side. At first it looked solid black, but then she turned to say something to the guy behind her and revealed the back of the shirt. We saw the swoopy logo that looked like a needle-nosed bird with its wings swept back, and underneath it, five words. Five awesome, magical words.

We Are the Sandpiper Network

I think Eric and I both tried to say either "whoa" or "dude" or something, but what we actually said sounded more like "WUUURRGGGHHHHHUUUUHHH," which makes no sense at all, but *whoa, dude!*

"Calm down, guys, she's way too old for you," Emily Barshaw

said from the seat in front of us, which was actually a helpful reminder that our plan was still supposed to be secret.

"Actual, real-life Sandpiper Network people!" I whispered.

"Who aren't us!" Eric whispered back.

"I totally want one of those T-shirts!" I was practically drooling. "Where did they get the T-shirts??"

"DefenderCon, obviously." Eric elbowed me (not hard) as he pointed toward the sidewalk. "You have to see this!"

A group of people in costume were walking away from World of Amazement, which looked hard to do just because they had to fight their way through the entire flow of foot traffic *toward* World of Amazement.

"Do you think they actually went into World of Amazement in costume?"

"It sure looks like it. Check it out, that Cloudsplitter costume is incredible," Eric said with deep envy in his whispery voice. "The helmet is perfect!"

"I like the guy dressed as Ogremeister too—the cross really looks like it's levitating between the antlers."

"And that club is huge."

There was also a tall girl dressed as Whirlybird, and a guy in a really good Shellshock costume. The grooves in his turtle shell lit up with exactly the right neon-blue glow. All four of them had super-happy smiles on their faces, and it seemed like they were high-fiving everyone in the crowd as they slowly cut through it in single file. A second later we lost sight of them, but by then we were too excited to care. Maybe we could talk to some of the DefenderCon people when we got inside World of Amazement!

UR EXCITEMENT LEVEL DROPPED
during the forty minutes it took to get from the
freeway to the actual parking lot, and when we
reached a big sign that said "Tour and Group Arrivals" some
people cheered again, but some said "finally," "took us long
enough," and other stuff like that. We were in a line of buses, all
of them full of kids, and all the kids in all the buses were eyeballing each other, scoping out the competition. Not in any kind of
hard-core way—a hundred band geeks staring each other down
isn't exactly terrifying—but still, everyone was curious.

World of Amazement has three hotels, if you can believe it,
and I felt giant pangs of envy when a handful of buses turned at
the big sign that said "Grand Palace of Amazement," which was
the fanciest of the three.

"My dad says the Grand Palace charges a person's immortal soul per night," I said.

"I believe it," Eric said. "I hear there are hot tubs and 120-inch TVs in every room."

"Yeah, so it's probably two immortal souls per night."

The next sign said "Wizard Castle of Amazement," which was definitely the best name out of all three hotels. More buses turned at that sign than at the sign for the Grand Palace, but still not that many. A minute or two later we got to the less-thrillingly-named Hotel of Amazement, where the remaining three-quarters of the buses turned in. The place looked weirdly retro from the outside, with a lot of pastel colors and a glittery sun-shaped thing on the roof that looked kind of like a disco ball. There was a much bigger "Hotel of Amazement" sign in front of the building, a blue rectangle shape with big, blocky letters that were all tilted a little differently from the others. It looked like something from a board game.

Whatever, though. When it was our turn to finally get off the bus, it was awesome, especially knowing that we didn't have to get back on for three days, even if it meant we'd have to be on guard for sneak attacks from assorted bullies. Everyone did a whole lot of stretching and wiggling around as the teachers talked to the hotel staff about unloading the uniforms and bigger equipment, then called off our names to grab our suit-cases. In the old days I would have brought my piccolo on the bus with me, but bass drums qualify as bigger equipment, so I didn't have to carry an instrument at all.

"You have reached your destination—the hotel for people without a ton of money," Eric said in a robotic voice.

"Roger that," I said in my own robotic voice. "Entering poor people's hotel in three, two—ow, hey! Skye, why—"

"Did your parents pay for this trip?" Skye said, completely ignoring the fact she'd just smacked me on the shoulder. She had a super-deadpan, "the Oh sisters are not here for your nonsense" look on her face.

"Er . . . yes?"

"What about you, Eric?"

"Well, yeah," Eric said. "Of course."

"Then you're not poor, so cut it out."

"You're so violent, Skye," I said. "I mean, it's kind of awesome, but—"

Skye ignored me and kept on walking. For a minute we just stood there watching her.

"Again with the bossiness," Eric said. "I hate it when she's like that."

"What, bossy? Or right?"

"Yes."

I cracked up. "Me too."

"Why can't she be more like her sister?"

"So now you have a crush on Summer Oh, eh?"

Eric snorted. "What are you talking about? *You're* the one who has a crush on Summer."

"*Had* a crush. The operative word is *had*, and that was last year. Plus, she also treats me like I'm her little brother, and I can't keep having a crush on someone who does that."

"Sure you can! Look at Skye!"

"Remind me why we're friends?"

"Now you just need to develop a crush on Graysin and you'll have, like, the Oh Sibling Triple Crown."

"Graysin's out of my league. And I like girls."

"Sure, but at least he doesn't treat you like you're his brother."

"MOOOOOOOOOOOVE," someone behind us yelled, and we hurried to catch up with Skye and everyone else who was in front of us.

The hotel looked old-school on the outside, but it didn't look old, as in old and broken-down. Up close, everything about it looked extremely shiny and new. The river of band geek lemmings washed up against the doors, and Eric and I went through the spinning doors even though the regular doors would probably have been faster, because why pass up the spinning doors if you don't have to? Then we were inside, where approximately 35 million kids were milling around like cattle headed to their doom.

Eventually we got herded into big, sloppy groups that were more or less near the line where all the teachers were getting us checked in. I caught a glimpse of Sean—he wasn't giving us the look of death anymore, which was a nice change. He did look like he was thinking really hard, though—his forehead was all wrinkled up, and he was tapping his mouth with the fingers of one hand.

"You know what, Sean's freaking me out," Eric said. "It doesn't even matter what he's doing."

"I'm sure he's planning our demise," I said.

"Dude, who actually uses the word 'demise'? Anyone?"

"I do."

"Well, yeah, you just did."

"It's a good word, you know."

"If you say so. Don't go to sleep on Kenny, though, he might be planning our demise too."

I sighed. "What is it about trumpet players?"

"Dude, be fair," Eric said. "Julie Forte plays trumpet, and she's awesome."

"Yeah, yeah, not all trumpet players."

"Okay, HILLTOP SUMMIT!" Mr. D said in his not-quite-shouting voice, waving at us as he walked backward toward a bigger, more open part of the lobby. "HILLTOP SUMMIT MUSICIANS, THIS WAY!"

The Hilltop Summit band geeks broke away from the larger swarm, and when we were all completely clear of the check-in lines Mr. D started calling out names.

"LISTEN UP! EMILY, ANA, MADISON, SUMMER! COME GET YOUR KEY CARDS!"

"That must be the eighth-grade genius room," Eric said as we slipped into the back of the Hilltop Summit mob.

"SKYE, GRACIE, EMMA, VIENNA!"

"And that must be the 'girls who do martial arts' room," I said.

Mr. D called up four or five more groups, and then it was finally our turn.

"MATT, ERIC, HECTOR, JACK!!"

"Awesome," Eric said.

"Yeah, let's go!"

We were so ready to get out of the lobby that we abandoned our usual evasion strategy and went right past Sean on our way up. I didn't realize he'd followed us until we'd walked away with our key cards in our hands and Mr. D had started calling out the next group.

"COLE, MALIK, ANDY, JAMES!"

"Room 622?" Eric said, holding up his key card, which was in a paper sleeve with "622" written on it by hand.

"Yup," I said.

"622!" Hector's grin was literally from ear to ear. Jack just nodded.

"Let's go!" I turned around, and Sean was standing so close behind me that my face almost collided with his face.

"Excuse you," he said.

"Ugh, what are you doing, Sean?" I said as I glared at him.

"Just waiting to find out my room."

"Enjoy," Eric said in a deadpan voice.

"Oh, I will," Sean said. He wasn't actively trying to block our way, but he didn't move out of our way either, so I started walking around him. *Then* he got in my way by walking directly in front of me, practically stepping on my feet in the process. I kicked his foot on purpose, and when he turned his head to glare at me, I pointed at Mr. Drabek, who was still handing out key cards, and cupped a hand next to my mouth, like I was about to call out to him.

"Snitch," Sean said with a sneer. "I was going over there anyway."

"Great, that works out, then!" I said, seething on the inside.

Sean didn't answer this time—his head came up like a dog spotting a squirrel, and he suddenly ran, not toward Mr. D, but past him.

"Man, what a jerk," Hector said. "What's his problem?"

"We'll tell you later," Eric said, sounding as annoyed as I felt.

The crowd of kids around Mr. D and the other teachers was shrinking as everyone got their room assignments, but there were still ten or eleven kids waiting. We were maybe twenty feet away at that point, and I looked around for Kenny—it's always a good idea to know his location. He was on the far side of Mr. D, just enough to the side so I could see him standing next to Sean.

Ruh-roh. Kenny wasn't using Sean as a punching bag—they were talking, in fact. That couldn't possibly be good.

Sean was saying something to Kenny with a hand in front of his mouth. Kenny turned his head and caught my eye *just* before a passing group of kids from another school got between us. The look on his face when he saw me was . . . not friendly. Really, really unfriendly.

What did Sean just say to him??

We walked across a section of the lobby that was full of long, low couches and super-brightly colored tables. Right after that we turned a corner into a sort of big hallway where the elevators were. There were eight elevators, and maybe a hundred people waiting, so it took a while for us to actually get the chance to try cramming ourselves into one.

Finally an elevator opened up right in front of us—well, right in front of the row of people in front of us, anyway. There was a whole lot of jostling around and bumping of suitcases as the elevator filled up, and in the shuffle I ended up being the last person in our group to get on.

I would have been the last person to get on the elevator, that is, if someone hadn't grabbed my backpack and pulled me back out. I yelped in surprise as I lost my balance—whoever the person was, they yanked me backward so hard that I actually left my feet. I only managed to avoid crashing to the floor because I spun to the side and got a hand down on the ground. Of course a hand clamped down on my shoulder, grabbed a fistful of my shirt, and started dragging me away from the elevators, which spun me around again so I was half stumbling and half falling. I whipped my head around in a panic, trying to see who had me, and of course it was Kenny.

"HEY!"

I turned my head back toward the elevators, and I saw Eric, Hector, and Jack pushing their way out, but they had to get past a couple of teenagers who'd crammed in behind them, and Kenny was really, really strong, and I couldn't keep my balance because we were going so fast. He dragged me away from the lobby and around a corner. A sign that said "Restaurant of Amazement" flashed in and out of my sight as I thrashed and kicked. I tried to grab the corner as Kenny hauled me around it, but my hands missed the corner's edge and slapped uselessly against the wall. I toppled backward again, and Kenny just kept dragging me along as I struggled to get my feet under me.

"LET ME GO!" I yelled. "ERIC, HELP!"

I heard shouting voices as Kenny hauled me past the entrance to the hotel restaurant and down a short hallway that ended at the bottom of a wide marble staircase.

Did they see us go this way? Did they see??

Kenny hauled me all the way up to a standing position, let go of my backpack, and spun me around by the shoulder, and as I flailed my arms to stop myself from falling, he punched me in the stomach. Hard. All the air went out of my lungs with a sound that was half grunt, half scream, and my legs felt like they'd turned into giant spaghetti noodles. I fell over on my side, trying desperately to catch my breath.

"You messed up, Wang!" Kenny's voice was terrifying—he sounded like he was possessed. "Thought it was funny to tell people I'm queer, huh?"

I took in a huge, whooping breath and looked up at him. "Wh-wh-what are you *talking* about?" I said as tears ran down to my chin. "I didn't—"

"*LIAR!*" Kenny roared. "You told *everybody*, but everybody knows *you're* the homo!"

He pulled back his fist to hit me again, but then he said "UNGH" as something or someone I couldn't see hit him from behind. A second later Eric basically wrapped himself around Kenny's whole arm so he couldn't punch me at all. I dragged myself to my feet as Kenny swung wildly behind him with his free hand, and he must have connected, because I heard an "OW" from behind him, and Hector staggered into view holding his ear.

Eric was still hanging grimly onto Kenny's arm, which turned out to be a mistake when Kenny used his other hand to punch Eric right in the face. Eric made a horrible yipping kind of sound, let go of Kenny, and fell on his back.

Eric! *Nobody messes with my best friend!*

"Hey, you boys!" a random adult voice said from over by the restaurant. "HEY, STOP!"

I launched myself at Kenny and threw a punch, but he just grabbed my fist out of the air and pretzel-bent my arm behind my back, which hurt a LOT. I screeched.

"Let him go, Kenny!" Hector yelled. I was bent over so I couldn't see what was happening, but Hector must have come at Kenny again and gotten hit again, because Kenny's body moved forward, which shoved me forward, and I heard Hector go "AGH!"

"What's wrong with you, Kenny?" I said. "I'm not the one who AAAAAAHH, OWW, THAT HURTS, OWWWWWW WW!!!"

"Stop it, Kenny!" Eric sounded like he was crying and shouting at the same time.

Kenny had his thumb dug into my wrist, and he was hitting a nerve ending or something because the pain was unbelievable. I almost lost my balance, which only made the pressure on my arm worse, and I screamed, boiling over with pain and terror.

"You don't get to talk about me at *all*, Wang," he snarled.

"AAAAAHHHHH—"

Kenny did something to my elbow that drove a spike of pain all the way to my wrist and shoulder at the same time. It felt like he was trying to pull the bones right out of my arm, and I screamed again.

"LET HIM GO!"

Mr. D. Finally.

Kenny suddenly let go and shoved me down hard. I went face-first into the floor, and my whole arm hurt so much that I had to roll over on my other side, cradle my hurt arm with my other arm, and push myself away from Kenny as fast as I could with just my feet.

"Move away from him, Kenny."

Kenny made a kind of huffing noise.

"NOW."

I backed up against the nearest wall and pushed myself into a sitting position. I didn't hear Eric come over next to me because all I could hear was the sound of myself crying, and I flinched when he touched my shoulder. I was glad he was there, though, and suddenly Hector and Jack were there too. Hector had a bump on his cheekbone that was already pretty big, and Eric's eye was puffy and red, but they were with me.

Kenny was backed up against the wall opposite from me, with Mr. D and another man in a blue jacket staring him down from a couple of feet away. The psycho-killer expression was gone from Kenny's face; now he just looked like he was bored to death instead of trying to beat me to death.

"Are you boys okay?" the man in the blue jacket said. Kenny snorted.

"Shut it, Kenny," Mr. D snapped. Kenny sneered, but he didn't say anything else.

"Yeah," Eric said, even though his eye was starting to turn seriously purple.

"Totally cool," Hector said, and he sounded totally cool when he said it, like nothing was bothering him at all.

Mr. D came over and knelt in front of us, and I let go of my hurt arm so I could wipe the tears off my face with the other arm.

"Matt, how's that arm?"

Kenny was looking right at me, so I stuck my arm out and bent it at the elbow, once, then twice. It hurt enough that I had to fight really hard to not show it, but no way was I giving Kenny any more satisfaction.

"It's fine," I said.

"You guys are pretty banged up," Mr. D said. "And that was a serious armbar, Matt—we shouldn't take any chances with your elbow and shoulder."

No. I'm not getting sent home because of Kenny. No. NO.

"He was pressing down on a nerve, Mr. D," I said, looking around at the guys for help. "It hurt, but it's totally feeling better already!"

Mr. D frowned.

"You've got full range of motion?"

I lifted my arm again and rotated it, which made my shoulder hurt, but less than bending my elbow made my elbow hurt.

"We're okay, Mr. D." Eric pointed at his own puffy-eyed face. "It's just a black eye."

"You can get a concussion from being punched in the eye, you know."

"Mr. D, it's all good!" Hector had somehow gotten himself into full-fledged super-cheerful mode even though it must have hurt his face to grin like that. "I mean, you gotta do something about Kenny, but we're good!"

Mr. D looked at us with that bushy-lipped frown still on his face, then looked down and chuckled, which is when I knew we were safe.

"Okay, but at least get some ice packs on those bruises."

We nodded seriously.

"What about *him*?" Eric said, pointing at Kenny.

"I'll deal with Kenny," Mr. D said. "You guys don't need to worry about him."

I blew out a long, shuddering breath, because it was a relief to know Mr. D was on it with Kenny, but I still felt wary, because you never know what else is gonna happen. You just never know.

**E FINALLY MADE IT INTO OUR**
room, feeling like we'd just lost a battle
with the Plutonium Brothers, and there
was no hot tub or wall-size TV, but there were two massive beds,
a desk, a couch, and a minifridge that we knew not to mess
with.

"My dad says the hotel charges you if you even breathe on the
little fridge," Hector said as we spread our stuff around the room
and flopped down on various pieces of furniture. Everyone else
flopped down, that is—I took my time sitting down just because
my arm still hurt.

"Yeah, no watching pay-per-view movies either—it's like forty
dollars per movie or something," Jack said in a totally serious

voice, and we all cracked up. We sounded a little hysterical, but who wouldn't have after being beaten up?

"I'm sorry I didn't get back fast enough," Jack said.

"What??" I said. "You're kidding, right?"

"Dude, Kenny was *murdering* us." Eric sat up and leaned toward Jack. "Going for help was a genius move."

"For real, Jack!" Hector got up and raised his hand to high-five Jack, which was the most Hector thing he could have done right then. "I mean, we could have taken him—"

"HA!" Eric and I said at the same time.

"—but you did the smart thing! Don't leave me hanging!"

Jack smiled and high-fived Hector. "Well, I wish I'd been faster."

"You were fast enough, Jack," I said seriously.

We didn't get to hang out in the room very long since the first event of the trip was an enormo-dinner with all twelve of the middle-school marching bands together. It turned out to be kind of fun. The food was awesome—really good burgers, super-crispy fries, and the thickest shakes I'd ever tasted—and we made the strategic choice to sit at a table within eyeshot of the teachers, which meant we were far, far away from anyone whose name rhymed with "Schmenny" and might want to punch us until we were dead. We spotted Sean at a table full of kids from other schools who were talking and laughing with him, not knowing all his secrets like we did. He was the only kid from our band at that table as far as I could tell.

I didn't see Kenny anywhere, and I wondered if he'd already been sent home. I hoped so.

Our table was great. We were across the table from Emily Barshaw and Nora Dairman, who got into a hilarious fake trash-talking session about reality cooking TV shows with some girls from another school. The insults were all stuff like "you'd put truffle oil on a roasted portobello burger" and "you think General Tso really invented General Tso's Chicken"—not insults, in other words. Although General Tso's Chicken definitely has nothing to do with the real General Tso.

As dessert (an amazing slab of chocolate cake) was being served, Eric leaned over and talked quietly into my ear.

"Since the competition's tomorrow, we should probably go review the plan for you-know-what tonight, huh?"

I nodded. "Definitely."

Hector and Jack went with a bunch of other kids to check out the hotel arcade while Eric and I, keeping a sharp eye out for hostile life-forms, headed back to the room.

"So that was a super-long day," Eric said as we took off our name badges and tossed them onto the desk.

"I know, right?" I said. "It was fun, but I'm wiped out."

"Yeah, I'm gonna put my pajamas on," Eric said with a yawn.

"Good idea. Review the plan, maybe watch some TV . . ."

"My thoughts exactly."

We were halfway through the pajama-putting-on process when we noticed the smell. Eric finished pulling a T-shirt over his head and sniffed the air.

"Do you smell that?"

"Yeah," I said, suddenly worried. "It smells like . . ."

"Something burning," Eric said. He turned around in a circle, still sniffing the air, and I had to grab his bare arm to get him to look at the door leading to the hallway. A thick gray haze was leaking into the room from around the door's edges.

Smoke! There was actual smoke coming into the room! And not just a little smoke—when I opened the door, thick gray smoke came pouring through it from floor to ceiling. I accidentally breathed in some smoke and went into a coughing fit so harsh that it felt like being stabbed in the lungs with a fork. Eric pulled me back from the door and kicked it closed. A second later the smoke detector over the door started beeping, and I mean really, really loud.

"There's a *fire?*" Eric said, rubbing my back as I choked and hacked. Eric sounded like I felt: completely freaked out.

I couldn't answer because I was doubled over, coughing harder than I'd ever coughed in my life. I thought I heard someone shouting out in the hallway, but it was hard to tell over the smoke alarm going off and the sound of me coughing up my own lungs.

"People are *screaming!*" Eric said, sounding panicked. "We have to get out of here!"

That was when smoke started pouring out of the bathroom.

We looked at each other in panic.

"THE BATHROOM IS ON FIRE!" Eric yelled. "LET'S GO!"

He ran to the sliding glass door and hauled it open. The smoke in the room swirled as fresh air came in through the open door. We scrambled out onto the balcony, quickly slid the door shut behind us, and backed up against the side of the balcony farthest from the door, panting. I looked around to see if I could spot any flames shooting out of the building—I couldn't really see very far up, but there wasn't any fire coming from the balconies on either side of ours. The fire alarm was still going off, though, and I could hear sirens in the distance.

I looked back at the glass door, wondering if we'd actually see the inside of the room go up in flames. That was when Eric grabbed my shoulder and I heard the sound.

Whap. Whap. Whap.

The room was too smoky to see anything that wasn't right up against the glass, so we couldn't see a face or even the outline of a body, but we could definitely see the open hand that was hitting the glass, fingers spread open, with a second or two between thumps. The hand thumped one last time, then suddenly darted sideways, toward the door handle.

"Wait a minute . . . ," I said, a horrible thought dawning on me. Eric must have had the same thought, because we both took a step forward with our hands reaching for the door. We were too late, though—before we even finished taking that first step forward, we heard something else.

Click.

It was the sound of the sliding glass door being locked from the inside.

Eric and I sprang for the door like a couple of crazed squirrels, grabbed the handle, and tried frantically to slide it open, but it didn't budge. We slammed our hands on the glass and yelled for whoever the person was to come back, but a whole bunch of loud voices seemed to burst into the air behind us, and when we spun around, pressed our backs to the glass door, and saw a crowd of people with glow sticks, drinks, and World of Amazement hats starting to gather, I suddenly got how dire the situation was.

"What do we do?" I said.

"You're asking me??" Eric said, darting his eyes in every direction.

Somewhere in the distance a fire engine started blaring its siren, which was only going to make the crowd of people bigger. We were locked out of our room, and the only way back inside was probably to jump off our balcony, run around to the front of the hotel, run through the lobby, take the elevator to our floor, and hope the door was still open. Which we couldn't do anyway, since our room was filled with toxic fumes. Either way, a *lot* of people would see us, which was going to be a problem, since I was wearing my Rocket Cats pajama pants and no shirt, and Eric was wearing a Sandpiper T-shirt and no pants, just his underwear.

People would take pictures for sure.

Our pictures would be *all over* the internet.

"Get down," I said in a low voice. We both sat down, then scooted around so our backs were against the side of the balcony wall, where we'd be less visible from inside *and* outside the hotel room.

"What are we gonna do?? I'm not wearing *pants*!" Eric said.

"I don't know. I don't know." Saying *I don't know* over and over wasn't helping, but I'd never seen Eric so panicked before, and I didn't know what to do. He was right; it wasn't that big a deal to have no shirt on, but no pants? If a picture of that made it online—heck, if someone even just talked about it online, he'd be teased and bullied about it until the end of time. Going to a new school in a different city probably wouldn't even save him. He laced his hands together and put them on top of his head and made a kind of high-pitched groan, and I couldn't stand it.

"Stay here, I'm gonna borrow something for you to wear."

"Matt. Nobody's going to let you borrow their PANTS," Eric said, putting some extra volume into "pants." It made it sound like he was mad at me, but I knew he wasn't.

"I know, but you could wrap a sweater or something around you. At least it would cover your undies."

Eric groaned again. "I guess, but who wears a sweater when it's this warm??"

Right. We were both half-naked, but I wasn't cold at all. I risked peeking up over the edge of the balcony, and I jerked back down when I saw how many more people were out there. If our balcony wasn't a couple of feet higher than the ground, they'd probably be climbing right up onto it. Or maybe not, since they probably thought the building was on fire.

The fire department, though. The fire engine siren was getting louder by the second, and when they arrived, the firefighters would be right on top of us, and Eric would be doomed.

I was NOT going to let that happen.

"I'll find someone who does. They're probably evacuating the hotel, so everyone will be outside. Don't worry."

"But all you're wearing is Rocket Cats pajama pants—"

He had a point—pictures of *me* would definitely be all over the internet—but that still wouldn't be as bad as underwear pics. Everyone at school already knew how much I loved the Rocket Cats.

Eric was my best friend. And if I didn't save my best friend from eternal online humiliation, how could I even call myself his best friend?

The fire engine siren was loud enough to make my ears hurt, and I peeked over the edge of the balcony again. The bad news was that the crowd of people was bigger; the good news was that everyone was looking in the direction of the siren. That was as good as it would get. There was a narrow strip of hedge I'd have to jump over, and I'd have to stand on the balcony wall to do it. I could do that. Maybe. Hopefully.

"Okay, it's now or never," I said, trying to sound less terrified than I felt.

"I just thought of something. What if the firefighters—"

"Keep low!"

"Matt, *wait*—"

I scrambled to my feet, climbed onto the top of the balcony wall (luckily for me, it was actually wide enough for that), tried as hard as I could not to look at anyone in the crowd, and quickly jumped. I cleared the hedge, braced myself for landing, hit the cement with both feet, and felt my ankle do something really, really wrong. There was a dull-sounding but sharp-feeling *SNAP*, a sudden kind of floppiness, and a gigantic bolt of pain that seemed to go all the way from one side of my ankle to the other. I fell over, howling, tried to stand up, and fell down again. A droning kind of numbness came over me, and I decided lying there on the cement was better than standing up, so that's what I did. I lay there, weirdly numb and in agony at the same time, and thought about how totally I'd failed to help my best friend.

A police officer suddenly appeared, looking down at me, then kneeling next to me.

"What's your name, son?" he asked. He seemed nice enough.

"Eric," I said.

"Try to relax, Eric. We've got a couple of EMTs on the way. They'll—"

"No, no, Eric's my friend," I said. "Can you help Eric?"

The cop looked back over his shoulder. "Is that your friend with the . . . what does that shirt say—"

"Sandpiper. Yes."

"He's all wrapped up in a blanket, but he looks like he's okay. My partner's talking to him."

A wave of relief went through me, and I must have moved my leg without thinking about it, because even though my ankle felt more and more like it was wrapped in a million layers of thick cotton, another zap of pain went through it. I yelped. Holy crap, it hurt.

That was okay, though. Someone had given Eric a blanket; there'd be no underwear pics of him online. People were probably taking a million pics of me and my Rocket Cats pajama pants, and it wasn't very comfortable lying there on the cement, but everything felt fuzzy and remote in a way that was weirdly pleasant, and Mr. D was suddenly there next to the cop.

"Hey, Mr. D," I said.

"Hi, Matt," he said, looking serious. *It's nice when teachers care*, I thought.

"Everything's kind of fuzzy," I said.

"That's probably because you're going into shock," Mr. D said. "Your ankle's pretty swollen. The EMTs are here, though, and I'm going with you."

"Where are we going?"

"The hospital."

And that was when it hit me: My ankle was messed up, and maybe even broken. I was going to the hospital, and probably home after that. Which meant there was no way Eric and I could go to DefenderCon. No way at all. Which was the thing that finally made me start crying.

It was all over. Our plan, which we'd worked so hard on and dealt with so much crap for, was a complete, humiliating failure.

OW DEPRESSING WAS IT TO LEAVE
the most fun place on the planet, not perform in
the biggest marching band event in the history of
the school, miss out on the only goodbye adventure I'd ever get
to have with my best friend, go to the hospital, get an operation
on my ankle that was broken in two places, and go home? Holy
crap, it was the most depressing thing *ever*. The only even slightly
good thing about it was the fact that I didn't have to lie to Mom
and Dad about breaking every rule in existence to go to DefenderCon with Eric, but even that was canceled out by the fact that
I didn't *get* to go.

I spent the next week at home letting the broken bones in my
ankle heal, getting used to the cast and the crutches, and learn-
ing lots of unpleasant, uncomfortable things about having a

broken ankle. For example, I had no idea how itchy your leg gets when it's sealed away in a cast, and how hard it is to scratch underneath a cast. It's obviously bad to scratch the place where the doctors cut your leg open in order to fix your ankle, so I spent a lot of time just letting it itch and screaming silently into the depths of my own brain. When it's hot outside, as it usually is in June, your cast will eventually start to smell, because having a broken ankle doesn't stop your leg from sweating.

I read a lot of books, which was nice, and watched a lot of TV, which was also nice, but I was bored and lonely, and I couldn't talk to Eric because for some reason he was in a massive amount of trouble. He called after I got home from the hospital, but he couldn't stay on the phone long because he was grounded and couldn't use his phone or computer for—

"The *rest of the school year*?" I could hardly believe it. "You're not serious."

"I am, though." Eric sounded more sad than I'd ever heard him. "It's actually even worse than that."

"How could it be any worse?"

"Dude, I can't tell you yet," Sad Eric said in his new Sad Voice. "Mom says you can come over one more time next week, though."

"*One* more time? That's so—"

"I know, Matt."

It felt like I'd been punched in the stomach again, only this time it wasn't Kenny, it was the whole universe.

"So . . . I guess I'll see you then."

I gulped.

"I guess."

"Just come over, okay? I'll be here packing and stuff like that."

"Okay."

So I waited for a week, then asked Mom for a ride to Eric's house. Getting my crutches into the car was way harder than you'd expect something like that to be, and I almost banged my leg against the car door as I got in, but eventually we got on the road. Eric's house was less than a mile away, so it only took us a couple of minutes to get there.

"Can you let me out here?" I said when we were at a stop sign a block away.

"Are you sure?" Mom looked both ways, went through the intersection, and pulled over.

"Yeah, I'll walk from here. Or crutch, I guess."

"It's still walking," Mom said with a smile. "You want it to be just you and Eric the whole time you see him, huh?"

"I guess."

"Okay." She reached over and petted my head. "Call me when you want me to pick you up."

"Okay."

"I love you, Matt."

"I love you too."

Getting out of the car was even more complicated than getting in, but after catching the tips of the crutches on eight different places inside the car, almost dropping a crutch into the gutter, and hanging on to the car while hopping over the gutter and onto the curb, I was safely crutching to the end of the block where Eric's house was.

That turned out to be harder than I thought, because by the time I stopped on the sidewalk in front of the house I was sweaty and winded, and my armpits kind of hurt. I stared at the truck in the driveway with "Eliopoulos Movers" printed on the side of it. It looked out of place, like it'd fallen from the sky and landed in the wrong alternative universe, but the two guys carrying a plastic-wrapped couch were definitely coming out of Eric's house. I watched as they angled the couch around the corner of the house and behind the truck.

Why was stuff already being moved out of the house?? There was still a week to go!

The guy in front was hopping up into the truck as I painfully crutched my way up to the front door, leaned one crutch against the door frame, and rang the doorbell. Since the door was still wide open, I could hear somebody doing something that involved a lot of crumpling paper sounds on the far side of the house, and I both heard and saw the feet that came running down the stairs, quickly revealing legs, arms, a body, and then all of Eric. He slowed down when our eyes met, walked the last four steps, and stopped at the bottom with his hand still on the banister. We stood there for about a hundred years, alternately looking at each other and looking everywhere else.

"Hi," I finally said.

"Hey."

I looked down, then looked up and started talking at the same time that Eric looked up and started talking.

"I'm—"

"I just—"

Well. That was awkward.

We stared at the floor some more.

"I'm glad you came over," Eric finally said.

"So am I." I almost crossed my arms, but had to stop when I almost fell over. My second crutch DID fall over, but Eric jumped forward and caught it before it hit the ground.

"Nice," I said as he slowly handed it back to me. "Thanks."

I hopped on my good foot as I got my crutches back under my arms.

"I better come in before I fall over," I said.

"Yeah, you better."

Eric stepped aside and flapped his hand like a matador, and I crutched past him into the living room.

"You're pretty good with those things," he said as I stopped at the sight of the mostly empty room.

"Yeah, I only fall down nineteen or twenty times a day," I said. "So . . . wow. Not much left in here."

"No. Most of the furniture's being sent in a truck tonight."

"Aren't you leaving next week?"

"No. We're leaving tomorrow."

"TOMORROW? What about the last week of school? And graduation?"

And your best friend?

Eric shook his head.

"When I got suspended, the principal said I could turn in all my final work by email. It's mostly written stuff."

"*When did you get suspended??*"

"I want to tell you about that, but let me just tell Mom what we're doing. She knows you're coming over, but she's practically got me under surveillance."

I let my brain marinate in that thought for a second, then looked around the room.

"Is there still furniture in your room, at least?"

"Yeah, the futon's still there. We're not taking that with us."

Eric's empty living room was a lot easier to navigate on crutches than our furniture-filled living room, and by the time he joined me I was already using his bedroom wall to lower myself onto his thousand-year-old futon. It sounded like he and his mom were having some kind of very serious conversation in the other room.

When Eric finally came into the room his face was way more red and splotchy than normal, but nothing was normal, so that made sense. Or didn't make sense? He flopped down on the futon next to me.

"Don't ask," he said before I could ask.

"Okay."

I took a deep breath.

"I'm sorry, dude, I—I didn't—"

"It's my fault," Eric blurted out in a wobbly voice. I was so taken by surprise that I stopped stammering.

"What, moving?"

"No. That." He pointed at the cast on my ankle.

I looked at my ankle and blinked.

"It's my fault you got hurt and our plans were wrecked. I'm really, really sorry—"

"What are you talking about??"

"You were trying to help me, remember? That's why you jumped off that balcony and got hurt!"

"*I'm* the one who decided to jump off that balcony. *You* tried to stop me, remember?"

"I'm the one who ran out onto the balcony with no pants on!"

"Well, yeah, that's true."

"Wait, what do you mean, that's true?"

"I'm just saying, grab some pants the next time we have to escape a burning hotel room."

"Dude. Maybe next time you shouldn't jump off balconies that are eight feet off the ground."

"It was *so* much higher than I thought it was."

We cracked up, and oh man, I felt such a huge wave of happiness, although it was all mixed up with sadness and regret too.

"I'm sorry I didn't call or email you or anything," Eric said quietly. "I couldn't."

"Yeah, I know. I didn't know you got suspended, though."

"Going out in a blaze of glory, right?"

"Did they blame you for the fire? Because if they did—"

"Oh no, that was Sean."

"WHAT? SEAN COMMITTED ARSON??"

I mean, come on. I didn't know if I could handle so many massive bombshells all at once. My head was in danger of exploding.

"Oh, no no no, it was a fake fire," Eric said. "He brought a couple of homemade smoke bombs on the trip and set one off right outside our room. He also put one in the air duct of our bathroom with some kind of timer. He's the one who locked us out on the balcony."

"How did he get into the roo—oooooohhhh, wait . . ."

An image of Sean talking to Kenny just before Kenny tried to kill me popped into my head.

"Sean set it all up, didn't he?"

Eric nodded. "Yeah. I guess Hotel of Amazement just gave

him a key to our room when he asked for one, which is why they're not suing the crap out of the school."

"Wow."

"Also, now everyone thinks that right after they stopped being friends, *Sean* started the rumor about Kenny making out with another guy, then told Kenny *you* started the rumor."

"Ooooh, I want to kill him. I want to rip his face off the front of his head."

"You and me both. Kenny was expelled, by the way."

"Good."

"Yup. Anyway, there are security cameras in the hallways with footage of Sean going in and out of our room, so he got caught."

"Wow." I shook my head. "He's really bad at that kind of thing, huh?"

"Ridiculously bad."

"It's a miracle he was able to plan the whole thing so far ahead without screwing it up," I said.

"Well, he did eventually screw it up."

"I guess so. It's good we didn't go to DefenderCon with him . . ."

I had to stop talking because of the huge lump that

materialized in my throat. We hadn't gone to DefenderCon without Sean either. We probably weren't ever going to DefenderCon.

"That's actually why I got suspended," Eric said.

"That's why you—are you kidding me? YOU WENT TO DEFENDERCON WITH SEAN?"

"Nooooo, not with Sean. The police arrested Sean—he's in even worse trouble than me. I went by myself."

?????

"Did you—" I sat up without thinking, remembered how hard it is to sit up without thinking when your ankle's in a cast, flailed my arms, and toppled over. Eric grabbed my shoulder and held me steady. His grin was fully in place, a great-white-shark kind of grin.

"Totally. I met Jonah Burns."

"HOLY CRAP! He was really there??"

I felt like I'd fallen in and sunk to the bottom of a swimming pool of envy.

"Yeah, he was super nice. Signed a comic for me and everything."

That snapped me out of it. Jonah Burns only signed one comic for my best friend? THAT JERK . . .

"What happened?? We had that whole list of different comics, we calculated how much everything would cost to buy, why didn't he sign all of them? Or at least TWO of them?"

"No, that's not—"

"Did he think we were gonna try to sell it all on eBay or something? I can't believe—"

"I only ASKED him to sign one thing because I only BOUGHT one thing."

I blinked.

"Why'd you only buy one thing?"

"It was kind of expensive."

"What, did you light the shopping list on fire and buy something else?"

"Kind of. Hang on a second."

Eric went to the closet and pulled out a backpack, which he zipped open as he sat back down.

"Here," he said, handing me a rectangular package wrapped in green and black paper. *Sandpiper's costume colors*, I thought.

"What is it?"

"Open it and find out."

I held the package up to my ear and shook it, which was stupid because it was obviously some kind of book. I sliced the taped-down edges of the paper with my thumbnail, opened the paper in mostly one piece, and stopped when I saw the cover of the book inside. The top half of it, anyway, which said "25th ANNIVERSARY OMNIBUS."

Gulp.

"Dude, is this—"

"Yup," Eric said with a grin.

I tore the rest of the paper off, knowing I'd see "SANDPIPER" in giant letters above a picture of Sandpiper herself, poised to leap off the roof of a skyscraper, silhouetted by a full moon.

"NO WAY."

"Totally way."

"Eric, this is out of control! Why—"

"Look inside."

The detail on the cover was incredible, so I admired it for a second longer before opening the book. I wanted to read the introduction, but I REALLY wanted to see the art credits on the splash page, so I started to flip ahead. Eric stopped me by putting a hand on top of the first page of the introduction.

"Look at the last page of the introduction first," he said.

I flipped ahead again, looking for the end of the introduction—it was a long intro. The last page of the intro had a final short paragraph, a single line that said "Art is everything" (Jonah Burns's standard tagline), another single line that said "Jonah Burns," and another paragraph of . . . handwriting?

Was that Jonah Burns's handwriting?

Hey, Matthew, Eric told me what happened to your leg—I'm sorry you couldn't make it today. Maybe this drawing will keep you company until you're back on your feet? I hope so.
All the best,
Jonah Burns

Under the autograph was a drawing of Sandpiper with a smile, a thumbs-up, and . . . a cast on her leg?

Jonah Burns had drawn what was definitely a one-of-a-kind portrait of Sandpiper with a broken ankle.

Autographed for me.

Just me.

The new lump in my throat was the size of a basketball, and I had to swallow hard to clear it.

"This is the limited edition omnibus," I said in a voice not much louder than a whisper. I couldn't stop staring at the autograph.

"Yup. The one with thirty extra pages of bonus content." Eric sounded so weirdly cheerful that I tore my eyes away from the book to look at him. He was grinning so hard that he looked like a cartoon character.

"They're only selling five hundred of them. They cost—"

"Kind of a lot, yeah. And they only had fifty of them at DefenderCon. I had to leave the hotel pretty early."

"So, what, you stood on line all day? And spent all your money on one thing?"

"Well, not *all* day. Just all morning."

"WHY??"

"Dude, why do you think?"

I lifted my shoulders in an awkward who-the-heck-knows gesture. Eric stopped grinning, leaned his head back against the wall, and looked at the opposite wall. He lifted a hand up to his shoulder, then snapped it forward and down while popping his index finger in the air.

"One, because it was fun going to DefenderCon, but it was also terrible going without you. Two, because you're the one who taught me about comic books, especially about Jonah Burns."

With each number Eric raised his hand and snapped it back down while popping out another finger.

259

"Three, we planned this together, but after you got hurt, this was the closest I could get to us going there together. Four . . ."

The emphatic hand motion thingy was slower this time.

". . . Four, I'm moving to a whole different part of the country."

Instead of raising his hand one last time, Eric stuck out his thumb so all his fingers were extended, starfish-style, and instead of karate-chopping that hand down, he used it to reach over, grab my shoulder, and gently shake me, his eyes still focused on the far bedroom wall.

"And five, you're my best friend. The best friend I've ever had, actually. I wanted to get something to, I don't know . . . help you not forget that we're friends."

I sniffled.

"I'm not going to forget," I said, trying not to sound too blubbery. "You're my best friend too."

"I know."

"I didn't . . . I didn't get anything for you," I said, feeling suddenly terrible about it. My best friend is going away and he gets ME a going-away present? How wrong is that?

"Sure you did. You came over here before it was, you know, too late."

A whole week down the drain. The last week of our friendship had just ended—gone, kaput, over—and I'd missed it. *We'd* missed it.

"I'm . . . I'm gonna miss you, you know," I said. "It's not like after you move we're gonna hang out a lot. Or at all."

"I'm gonna miss you too," Eric said. "I mean, you know, I love you and all that."

Suddenly we both had to look everywhere else in the room except at each other.

"M—me too. I . . . love you too."

"I know."

I snorted, but it was a more sentimental-feeling snort than usual.

"Sometimes I wish we were brothers," I said. "I know that's weird . . ."

"I've wished that too," Eric said. I glanced sideways at him, and he was smiling. "We can be, you know. Kind of. Not biological brothers, but, like, brothers by choice."

"Kind of like how my mom says 'found family'?"

"Yeah, like that. Found brothers."

"Yeah. That sounds . . . really good."

"We'll still talk, you know. Maybe your parents will finally get you a phone."

"Yeah, maybe, but it won't be the same."

"I know," Eric said. "But hey, we're hanging out now."

"This is . . . it's amazing," I said, holding up the book. "This is so . . . thanks. Have you read it yet?"

"Duh, no." Eric looked at me with an are-you-kidding look on his face, all raised eyebrows and twisted-up mouth. "It's a GIFT, Matt."

"We should read it now, right? Do you have to do moving stuff or anything?"

"Yeah, but not right away."

Good enough for me.

"You mind if we skip the intro?"

"Nope."

I smiled down at the autograph one more time, then flipped to the opening splash page, which was for a brand-new Sand-piper story, written and drawn by Burns just for this omnibus.

"OOOOOOOHHHHH, DUDE," Eric and I said in unison.

Sandpiper was leaping off a wall into what looked like a har-bor behind her, but she'd twisted her body as she jumped so she was facing back the way she'd came while bullets whizzed past her. Some kind of glowing orb was tucked under one arm, and her other arm was cocked over her head, ready to hurl a Stinger at whoever was shooting at her. It was a classic Sandpiper pose—perfectly balanced, fearless, and ready to strike.

"This is incredible," I said.

"The best," Eric said.

We leaned into each other to get a really good look at the details, and for a second I thought about the hundreds of times we'd read comics together, which was usually us reading separately, but not always. So this wasn't the first time we'd read the same comic together, but it was probably the last.

I blinked twice, hard, not wanting to make Eric wait for me because I couldn't read through my own tears. I guess it wasn't just me, though, because he started to talk, but then had to stop and clear his throat.

"Is that Whirlybird?" he said. The wobble was back in his voice.

"That is totally Whirlybird." I sniffled and rubbed the back of my hand across my eyes, fast and hard. Whirlybird was Sandpiper's early crime-fighting partner turned longtime nemesis.

"That's a new costume, isn't it?"

"I think so."

"Awesome."

"I can't believe you got this for me."

"Believe it."

I did, actually. When I thought about it, it was no surprise coming from my best friend.

"I believe it," I said in a low voice, almost to myself.

And I flipped to the next page, because the best thing about a Jonah Burns comic is that even when things are totally going wrong for Sandpiper and it's scary or weird or even sad, even if she was about to lose someone she cared about, I still wanted to find out what happened next.

ACKNOWLEDGMENTS

THE BOYS IN THE BACK ROW ISN'T AN AUTO-biography, but the friendship it's inspired by is very real. Thanks to Chris Eliopoulos, my fellow drummer and superhero enthusiast of old, for the gift of friendship that eventually led to the creation of this book. This is really something, isn't it, Chris? We're still here, we're still friends, and I'm so glad.

It's an honor to be among the very first authors published by Levine Querido, and my appreciation for the stellar work and buoyant spirits of Antonio Gonzalez Cerna, Alexandra Hernandez, Meghan Maria McCullough, and Nick Thomas is boundless. I mention Arthur A. Levine separately because come on, it's Arthur. He's the best of editors and the best of friends, and this is a story we were meant to work on together.

Thanks to Dion MBD for a cover illustration that so

thoroughly captures the spirit of friendship I was aiming for, and to Chad Beckerman for a design that pops and zings in all the best ways. I have a giant oak aging barrel of respect for the people of Chronicle Books and the work they'll do to get my book out into the world.

My endless gratitude goes to agent extraordinaire Ammi-Joan Paquette, whose guidance and knowledge were essential in getting both *The Boys in the Back Row* across the finish line and my career out of the starting gates. The same goes for all my friends in the Erin Murphy Literary Agency community, whose love and support has truly meant the world to me.

Ellen Oh, Martha White, Ann Braden, and Olugbemisola Rhuday-Perkovich read early, preposterously untidy drafts of this book, and their literary acumen and insight stuck with me the rest of the way. Charlie Nelson generously shared his insider knowledge on the sequence of events that would follow the deployment of a hotel fire alarm.

Finally, and most importantly, all my love goes to Miranda, Zoe, and Leo. They're more than just my support system (although Miranda does more to support my career than everyone else on Earth combined), and they're more than just my connection to the panoramic weirdness of life during childhood (although Leo and Zoe are the most riotously joyful connections I could ask for). They are the people in this world who I love and cherish more than all others, and I'd be neither the person nor the writer I am today without them.

SOME NOTES ON THIS BOOK'S PRODUCTION

The jacket illustration was created by Dion MBD using Procreate. First, it was sketched in grayscale silhouette to determine the composition and lighting. The final linework was drawn on top of the magnified sketch, and then it was colored. To finalize the piece, prescanned textures were layered onto the illustration. The text was set in Adobe Garamond, designed by Robert Slimbach in 1989. It was based on a Roman type by sixteenth-century Parisian engraver Claude Garamond and an italic type by Robert Granjon. The display type, Gotham Bold, was designed by American type designer Tobias Frere-Jones in the early 2000s. Initially commissioned by GQ magazine, the Gotham typeface was inspired by Frere-Jones's walks through New York City, and the lettering he admired on older buildings. It was composed by Westchester Publishing Services in Danbury, CT. The book was printed on 98gsm Yunshidai Ivory FSC™-certified paper and bound in China.

Production was supervised by Leslie Cohen and Freesia Blizard
Book jacket and interiors designed by Chad W. Beckerman
Edited by Arthur A. Levine

LQ
LEVINE QUERIDO